Nancy Brandon's Mystery

By

LILIAN GARIS

Author of

"NANCY BRANDON"

WHITMAN PUBLISHING CO.

RACINE, WISCONSIN

Printed in the United States of America

CONTENTS

CONTENTS

NANCY BRANDON: IDEALIST

CHAPTER I

JUST A LITTLE LOVE

They both were carefully folding garments —Nancy sort of caressed the few dainty little silk things while her mother placed tissue paper between the folds of her tan tailored skirt, and then laid it gently in the steamer trunk.

"I can't help feeling a little guilty, Nancy dear," she murmured. "To go all the way over there without my darling daughter." The next garment was laid down, and two loving eyes encompassed the girlish figure before her.

"You know I wouldn't go, anyway," Nancy bravely answered. "I'm going to save my trip to Europe, until—until—later," she faltered.

"You shall have it," declared her mother firmly, "and only the importance of this trip to my business—"

"Of course I know that, Mums," and Nancy forgot the packing long enough to fold two prompt arms about her mother's neck. "You'll come back so wise with all your foreign cataloging, that you'll be made chief of the reference department. Then I'll go to college—maybe; although I would so much rather go to art school."

The young mother smiled indulgently. "College will not interfere with your art ambitions, dear," she explained. "But there's time enough to decide all that. What's worrying me now, is leaving you for this long, unknown summer."

"That's just it," Nancy hurried to add. "It is unknown. It seems to me everything happens in summer. Winter is just one school-day after another, but summer! What can't happen in summer?"

Dancing around with a wild pretense of gaiety, Nancy was dropping this article and picking up that, in her efforts to assist with the European packing; but even the most uninformed stranger would easily have guessed that the impending separation was disquieting, if not actually alarming to her, as well as to her mother.

Mrs. Brandon, Nancy's mother, was being sent abroad in the interest of an educational quest, being carried on by the library which employed her; and besides Nancy there was Ted. Ted the small brother, so important and so loving a member of the little group. But summer for a boy like Ted merely meant the selection of the best camp, with the most trustworthy counsellor and the best established reputation. That, with his little trunk, his brown suits and his endless wood's-tools, made up Ted's schedule and outfit, without a possible flaw in the simple arrangements.

Not that he didn't sniffle, as Nancy whispered to Miss Manners, because he did, every single time he looked at the last picture he, Nancy, and his mother stood against the old tree for, while Manny snapped it.

More than that, Nancy had seen him take Nero, his dog, down to the pond twice in one day, the day before he left for camp, although Nero could not have needed two baths, with soap and a rub down, in one day.

But Ted was gone now, and there remained but one more night and two hours of the next day before Mrs. Brandon also should be gone.

The thought was appalling. Gone for two whole months while Nancy would be visiting her rich but unknown cousin Rosalind.

The day before any important event is usually a time of anxiety or of joyous expectation, for the joy, or even the fear of anticipation, is a well known preliminary condition. So it was this which Nancy and her mother were experiencing.

The daughter was by no means an unusual girl, for all girls are remarkable in their own peculiar way. Nancy was dark, her eyes having the same tint as her hair—when one regarded their mere color, but looking into them or having Nancy throw out their full powers upon another, gave the quiet little pools such glints and flashes, that their color scheme became quite secondary in actual valuation. Laughter seemed to wait in one corner while concern was hidden just opposite, for Nancy Brandon was a girl of many moods, original to the point of recklessness, defiant of detail where that might interfere with some new and novel idea, but always sincere.

It was this last saving quality that endeared Nancy to her many friends, for who can resist a perfectly honest girl, unselfish, and unspoiled? Her prettiness was a matter of peculiar complement, for being tall she was correspondingly thin and supple, being dark she had a lovely olive skin with little patches of rose color, and her hair—well, her hair had been long, curly, and her mother's pride, but Nancy was now determined to have it bobbed —some day soon!

"It is not only old fashioned," she had argued with her mother, "but barbaric. American girls are not going to be ape-ish any longer. You'll see."

To which the mother had listened reasonably and had given Nancy permission to get her hair cut if she chose—after she reached the summer home of her cousin Rosalind. This qualification of the much argued plan was so fixed because Rosalind had wonderful hair and, said Mrs. Brandon, Nancy might not like to be without any, or much, in contrast.

"I suppose it will be queer in the big house," Nancy interposed without need of elucidation. "Big houses always are queer and—spooky."

Mrs. Brandon laughed lightly at that. "I'm glad you're not timid, Nance," she said, "for the old place must seem rather uncanny by this time. But it was beautiful, very beautiful when your Aunt Katherine lived. Of course, Aunt Betty is so much younger—"

"And a step-wife to Uncle Fred," jerked Nancy. "I always think that step-wives are up-ish and put on a lot of airs. I'm sure Rosalind thinks so too."

"You mean second wife to Uncle Fred and stepmother to Rosalind," corrected Mrs. Brandon. "Rosa is just about the age to be rebellious—"

"And she's so—awfully fat."

All this was merely the going over of well known details, concerning the big house and its occupants, forming the background of Nancy's prospective summer. For she was to visit Rosalind Fernell at Fernlode, in the New Hampshire mountains, and Rosalind was best known as being "awfully fat." True, she was also step-daughter to Mrs. Frederic Fernell, the lovely little and very young wife of Mr. Fernell of the famous woolen mill company. But to Nancy, Rosalind seemed unfortunate because of both these conditions; being fat and being a step-daughter were inescapable hardships, thought she.

Letter after letter had poured out Rosalind's miseries, in fact it was because her troubles were presented by the cousin as being really acute, that Mrs. Brandon hesitated long before deciding to let Nancy visit her. But the big hearted Uncle Frederic, in his letters pointed out what appeared to be the real truth of the situation, namely: that Rosalind was rather spoiled from being alone so much, and, of course, Betty, his young wife, couldn't possibly make a companion of a little spoiled child, so—

"I'm sure to love Rosalind," Nancy again reflected, "because she seems so frank and honest. Being fat isn't a crime. She can't help that." This decision, merely a repetition of her usual conclusion, was being reached as a sequel to Uncle Frederic's last letter.

"Mother," Nancy began, bravely attempting to banish the loneliness that even now seemed to foreshadow herself and her charming young mother, "do tell me once more, just *once* more, about Orilla. Is she Rosalind's cousin?"

"No. Orilla is really the daughter of a nurse who was with Uncle Fred's first wife, your Aunt Katherine, during her long illness. Orilla lived at Fernlode, and naturally felt it should always be her home. In fact, she even felt that she should have been the proverbial Cinderella, but there was no such idea in the minds of Uncle Fred or Aunt Katherine.

Mrs. Rigney, Orilla's mother, had been very generously paid for her services, and Orilla's education was also provided for; but the girl seems to hold a bitter grudge against your new Aunt Betty—quite as if uncle Fred's marriage to her had cut off Orilla's hopes, you know."

"Oh, yes," murmured Nancy. "I can understand that. But I don't see why Rosa bothers with her."

"She is, I believe, a rather persistent young lady and it is she who bothers Rosa. However, dear, don't you worry about that angle of Uncle Fred's affairs. Just make up your mind to have a wonderful time and so soothe my conscience for leaving you."

Followed moments, minutes, little hours of tender endearments. The mother cautioning, telling, advising, reminding Nancy of so many and such various possibilities; the daughter questioning—just that, and only with the loving look from the soft, dark eyes, the appeal from her trembling lips, the protection begged by her eager young arms; for Nancy was now quite conscious of the fact that her mother, the great, the wonderful fortress against every possible and every impossible evil, was about to be withdrawn from her life for a time. But time didn't seem to matter. Two months or two years; it was just the fact, the unavoidable disaster that confronted her.

"Your hat box holds as much as a suitcase," said Nancy, laying very tenderly into the round, black box, one more pair of nice, white silk stockings, Nancy's extra gift. "Be sure to wear your black and white felt on the steamer, Mums. You look stunning in that hat."

"All right, sweet-heart, I'll remember," promised the mother, who herself was busy with Nancy's things. "I'm glad your trunk goes today. Somehow it is easier to attend to mine—"

"Oh, yes. Hum-m-m-hum. You want *me* out of the way first. But, really, I think it cheating not to let me see you off," grumbled Nancy in pretty pretense.

"Now, you know, dear—"

"'Course I do. I'm just teasing you, Mumsey. I wouldn't really want to get mixed up with your party. They might sweep me away and put goggles on me, to match me up with the library high-brow folks. When a girl's mother is made a librarian delegate, I suppose," sighed Nancy affectedly, "she ought to wear goggles anyway."

"Don't go making fun of my—peers," cautioned Mrs. Brandon in the same bantering manner. "I tell you, my dear, if it were not for the library we wouldn't any of us be taking a vacation. There's the postman now. And I can see Ted's postcard coming!"

"Four of them!" shouted Nancy, who had already made hold the bright pictured messages. "Why four, all at once?"

"Laid over," laconically answered the postman. "Those camps let their mail pile up, I'll tell you."

But Nancy was deciphering the boy's scrawl which, when classed as handwriting, was never model, but now, classed as his first message home from his first week at camp, amounted to perfectly ideal "broad-casting."

They read and re-read, Nancy finding little secret words sticking on the canoe sails and peeping out of, what might have been a cloud-burst, if the postcard had not carried with it the other explanation. This read "Beautiful Lake Tuketo by Moonlight" and it was the moonlight effect that was so apt to be misleading.

"He's all right, at any rate," remarked the mother, thus betraying her anxieties. "And he seems to be having a good time," she sighed relievedly.

"Trust Ted for that," Nancy reminded her. "But what an awful looking lot of boys! Just see my card! They look like a comedy parade."

"Why Nancy! They're fine looking little chaps, I'm sure," defended Mrs. Brandon. "But I suppose that picture was taken to show the raising of Old Glory, not as a beauty contest illustration."

" 'S'cuse me," murmured Nancy. "Of course, they're—darlings, every one of them, but I wouldn't swap our Ted for—the whole bunch!"

"Nancy—Brandon!!"

"Yes-sum!" confessed Nancy, glorifying in her pretended ungrammatic freedom.

CHAPTER II

AN INCIDENTAL EXPLOSION

Even the most difficult tasks are finally accomplished, and now Nancy was actually riding towards Boston. The details of closing up their little home had been rather confusing, especially as each member of the small family was starting out in a different direction, but it was all done at last, and soon Nancy would cross Boston and take the Maine line out toward New Hampshire.

It seemed so unnecessary for any one to meet her at the South Station and taxi with her over to the North Station, but there was Miss Newton, a friend who had visited the Brandons and who lived almost in Boston. With her, Nancy's mother had arranged, both for crossing the big city and having lunch, so that there could be no possible danger in her daughter's journey. Also, after lunch in the upstairs station restaurant, Miss Newton, a lively young woman who seemed just like a girl to Nancy, insisted upon making up a little box of fruit for the train journey.

"Never can tell about these long afternoon rides," said Miss Newton, when she bought five more blue plums. "They may side-track you and you'll be glad to have a fruity supper along with you."

Nancy expressed her gratitude, of course, and as the Boston and Maine afternoon train steamed out, she didn't feel quite so lonely without her mother, because of Miss Newton's jolly waving and pleasant little send-off.

The train was crowded. Many mothers and children seemed to have been on shopping tours. Naturally Nancy was concerned with the prospect before her, for since Rosalind's letters were so effusively pre-welcoming and so hysterically anxious about what she termed, "the troubles and trials at Fernlode," Nancy could form no opinion of the strange household. She knew she was going to be shy of that important new, stylish, beautiful Aunt

Betty, for the reputation she had obtained was enough to strike awe into the heart of any girl visitor. Of Uncle Frederic she knew positively that she just loved him, for he had visited her own home late last fall, and he was "a king" as Ted expressed it. Rosalind had been away at boarding school all the time, it seemed to Nancy, so the young cousins had never met, for even Rosalind's vacations had been usually spent abroad. This year, however, she had insisted upon remaining at home, although her father and step-mother were to sail shortly.

But now Nancy's train sped on, and the flying landscape, though novel after the big factories and the bridges were passed, held small interest for the young summer tourist. She noticed that a woman with two small boys had bought those silly little boxes of ice-cream with the foolish tin spoons, and their delight in lapping up the stuff was rather amusing. It was funny, too, to see the people spill water cups along the aisle, and when a very stout man dozed off, and let his bald head tap a lady on her bead-bedecked shoulder, Nancy indulged in an audible titter while the ice-cream boys shouted loud enough to wake up the indecorous gentleman.

Such trifling incidents helped to while away the time, and after the big mill dam was passed, which according to the timetable indicated the state line of Massachusetts and New Hampshire, with somehow touching on a corner of Maine, then Nancy knew the journey was almost over.

The afternoon was cool and pleasant, for early June was still behaving beautifully, and Nancy was not sorry that she had taken her mother's advice and worn her school suit of blue serge.

"I suppose," she ruminated, "Rosalind's clothes will be gor-gee-ous." This visioned her own limited outfit. "But being so fat it must be hard getting clothes. They all have to be made to order, of course."

It was at this juncture that the little old-fashioned woman, in the seat opposite Nancy, spread her ginghamed self out in the aisle, in order to cope more freely with the over-crowded bag she was struggling to close. Her efforts were so violent, and her groans so audible, that everybody around took frank notice of her. First, she would get between the two seats, backing to that in front, and trudge away at the helpless, hopeless carry-all. Then, she would put the bag on the floor and work from the aisle. Finally, she literally threw up her hands and looked comically at Nancy.

"Ain't it the mischief, sissy?" she said suddenly. "I got to get off with that bag bulged wide open."

Nancy laughed outright. "Sissy" was such an old-fashioned name to be called. Then she looked critically at the recalcitrant bag.

"Maybe I could do it," she suggested, although she instinctively felt like calling the car man to help. Yet the funny little country woman, with her checked gingham dress, her bronzed skin and her perfectly useless hat, that merely rested on the top of her frowsy head, was smiling so friendly, that Nancy felt impelled to offer personal aid.

So she stepped over and tackled the bag. It was too full, much too full, of course, and the articles in it were the non-crushable kind, hard and firm. Surely the biggest opponent to the catch and its clasp meeting was a bottle, for it bulged out in one place as fast as Nancy tried to push it in at another.

"I'm afraid I can't close it," Nancy admitted reluctantly. "Couldn't you take anything out?"

The woman pulled her face into such funny crinkles, it looked as if she was winking all over it. Then she made queer noises, but they could not be called words, and at last a man who had been watching the performance, over his reading glasses, dropped his paper and silently offered his services.

He was a very dignified gentleman, and he readily acknowledged Nancy's presence, although he did not directly address her. The little woman was being regarded as very much out of order, and truth to tell she was very generally disturbing the peace in that end of the car.

But now the man, with his strong hands and white shirt-cuffs, undertook to conquer the rebel bag. He would plainly have no nonsense, would make short work of it, for his face was set with a look of active determination.

Once, twice, he tried to snap it shut. Then —there was something like an explosion!

Splash! A perfect fountain of red liquid shot straight up in the air!

"Oh, mercy!" yelled the owner of the bag. "There goes Martha's grape juice!"

And go it did, apparently as far and farther than even good home-made grape juice is supposed to travel, for it covered the face and shirt front of the determined man, it all but shampooed the blonde head in the next seat front, it managed, somehow, to include Nancy in its area, for across the aisle shot a thin but virulent little stream, and while one party was trying to dodge it another would fall into its furious path.

"A bomb! A bomb!" yelled one of the ice

cream boys joyfully.

"Maybe it's a bandit's hold-up," yelped the other boy, hopefully.

"It's my lovely grape juice and it's working—" moaned the woman in the gingham dress. But what she meant by "working" was not what the spectators were thinking of. She meant effervescing, while they simply saw liquid fireworks shooting around the car.

It was all over in a few moments, but the well intentioned man could not erase the stains from his expansive shirt front—it was hard enough to get the grape juice out of his eyes.

The blonde woman, whose bobbed head had been caught in the shower, seemed the one most injured, and she took no trouble to restrain her indignation!

"The idea! Carrying that stuff around!" she argued. "Just imagine! Black and blue grape juice," and she swabbed her head frantically with all the handkerchiefs she could resurrect from pockets and hand bags. Blonde hair dyed wine color did look odd.

"I'm awfully sorry," the gingham woman admitted. "It was just a present from my cousin Martha—"

"Then, why didn't you hire a truck instead of buying a railway ticket," fired back the crimson-spotted blonde. "Seems to me—" But her further arguments were lost in the sudden stopping of the train and the hurried getting off of the unfortunate grape juice owner.

She made opportunity for a smile to Nancy, however, as she edged her way out, and as she left the train it was the boy who had shouted "bomb" at the accident who pegged her the cork of that bottle. Strange to say, the woman caught the stopper, and bravely took the almost empty bottle from the rebellious bag, banged the cork in firmly, and was then on her way—with the bottle in one hand and the famous bag in the other.

Everyone's face seemed to betray amusement, for during the entire episode the little woman had shown real good nature. First, she was patient, as well as determined, in attempting to close the obstreperous bag; next, when the mighty all-knowing man went to her assistance and caused the grape juice explosion, she only smiled and herself took the blame for his mistake.

All of this wavered in Nancy's mind, and with it came one of those unaccountable little flickering thoughts, unbidden and unreasonable. It suggested a future meeting of Nancy and the gingham woman.

"But wherever would I and why ever should I meet her again?" Nancy deliberated. "She's probably just some farmer lady, and this station is miles from Craggy Bluff."

The incident served admirably to brighten the last hour of her journey, and even the wonderful capers of a late afternoon sun, gyrating over the New England hills, failed to hold interest now, as a long train trip wound up the miles, like a boy's fish line after a long waiting and a poor catch.

Nancy's bag and hat box were made hold of even before the trainman called out the station, and now that she had actually arrived at Rosalind's summer place, Nancy caught her breath, apprehensively.

"With mother in Europe and Manny far off, I'll have to like it," she reflected, "but then, why shouldn't I?" Her question poised itself boldly before her, for somehow even the lure of luxury was not altogether reassuring.

It was now almost seven o'clock, and the young tourist noticed no one preparing to leave the train at the approaching station. True, there were so few passengers left, there might be individual stations for each one of them; but Craggy Bluff was sure to be exclusive.

The very word as she thought of it, rather terrified Nancy, for, after all, she enjoyed folks, loved companionship and appreciated girlhood's privileges.

"But Rosalind and—Orilla," she was forced to reflect, "they will be good company—I hope." It was Orilla's personality that puzzled her, for the accounts of that queer girl had been anything but flattering.

"Craggy Bluff!" called out the trainman,

who promptly approached Nancy and took up her bag. This had been arranged for by the thoughtful Miss Newton, when the train was leaving Boston, so that there was no danger of Nancy mistaking her destination, or being inconvenienced by her baggage.

She stepped from the train, thanked the trainman and took her bag, just as a smiling girl ran up to her.

It was Rosalind! Fat and rosy, jolly and rollicking.

"Nancy!" she cried happily.

"Rosalind!" responded the traveller.

"Oh, how ducky! I just couldn't wait. Over here. Chet!" called Rosalind to the chauffeur, who promptly hurried along for the bags. Rosalind continued to puff and putter. "Nancy! Isn't it too darling to have you come?" Her arm was wound around Nancy's waist. "Do you like the woods? And the water? And the hills? We even have wild beasts out here, but I never have hunted alone. Here's our car. Jump right in. Chet, I must call at the post office." Thus rattled on the exuberant Rosalind, as Nancy formed her first pleasant opinion of the important cousin.

Following these preliminaries, Nancy did manage to say a few words. But they didn't mean anything, much, other than being pleasant words happily spoken.

The cousins were at last becoming acquainted, and while Nancy knew she was sure to love the impulsive Rosalind, Rosalind felt she was simply "dead in love" with Nancy, all of which favored the hopeful summertime ahead.

CHAPTER III

COUSIN AND COZ

Winding in and out of wooded drives and tree tunneled roads, as they went from the station, Nancy sensed something of the luxury she had so wondered about.

Yes, it was wonderful to cover distance that way, and the distance itself was wonderful, because Craggy Bluff was one of those works of Nature varied in detail from the finest ferns to the shaggiest giant oaks, and the very craggiest gray granite rocks to the daintiest pearl pebbles that studded the silvery beach.

"Oh, such glorious trees!" Nancy would exclaim as the car tore holes in the sunset's shadows.

"Trees! If you like trees, Nance, just wait until daylight, and I show you huge black forests," declared Rosalind, kindling merrily to Nancy's enthusiasm.

"And when Uncle Frederic and Aunt—his wife," Nancy corrected herself, "go away, will you be here all alone?"

"All alone! I wish I could be," replied Rosalind, "then we could have sport; just you and I and, of course, a few servants. But, Nance, I never can get away from Margot, my old nurse, you know. Darling mother, my own mother, trusted her always, because she herself had been ill so long, so, of course, Margot's sort of bossy yet. She's as good as gold, but one doesn't want gold bands around one's neck all the time," laughed Rosalind, as the car drew up to the broad veranda.

Even in the dusk, for it was now quite dark under the heavy foliage, Nancy could easily discern the massive outline of the big country house. She knew its story; how her Uncle Frederic had bought it from some old New England family just because it offered a seeming refuge for the first Mrs. Fernell, Rosalind's mother, whose early invalidism had ended in leaving the girl so much alone among servants and wealth. Aunt Katherine had loved the big house which she had called Fernlode, because the ferns grew in paths and veins almost unbroken in their lines, and also because Fern was a part of their old family name.

"Here we are, Margot!" called out Rosalind, as a big woman came up smiling to that call.

She greeted Nancy happily, and at once the visitor understood why she was considered bossy, for she directed the man to take the bags and to do several other things all at the same time.

"Rosalind dear, you should have worn a sweater. See how cool it is—"

"A blessing, Margot dear. Haven't we been roasting for days? Sweater! I just want to feel comfortable for a little while. Come on, Nance, I always run upstairs. Helps me reduce—"

And the puffing Rosalind executed a series of jumps, in lieu of running, which seemed too much to expect of her, and this bore out the fat girl's good intentions.

"I do every earthly thing I can, you know," confessed Rosalind, as they stood before an open door, "but I can't see that it does one bit of good. I'm—hoping—you may have—a secret—recipe—" Breath giving out, Rosalind gave in, and sank down on a big chintz covered chair.

"I don't see why you worry about being fat, Rosa," said Nancy with real sincerity. "Here I'm too thin and mother keeps worrying about that all the time—"

"Oh, what an idea!" chuckled Rosalind. "We can be the Before and After sign—fat and thin, you know. Wouldn't that be great?" and as she laughed Nancy remembered another familiar sign. It was to do with laughing and growing fat!

"Shall I change for dinner?" Nancy asked when the gale of mirth subsided and Rosalind stood before a mirror patting her turbulent hair.

"No-o-o!" drawled Rosa. "Just put a ribbon around your head and that'll be all you need to do. Dad won't be home tonight—

he's in Boston, and Betty" (she whispered this) "is never home when Dad's away. So a ribbon will fool Margot, and after dinner—" A queerly pulled face, that made a pincushion out of Rosa's features, finished the sentence. Evidently she had some important plans for after dinner.

As they "fussed up" Nancy noticed how really pretty Rosalind was. Her eyes were always laughing and they were blue, her mouth was always smiling and it was scalloped, and her hair was "gorgeous," being a perfect mop of brown curls rather short but not bobbed. It was this head of hair that from baby hood had distinguished Rosalind, for her "lovely curls" were a matter of family pride to all but herself.

Her weight, however, could not be denied, even by one so favorably prejudiced as Nancy, for Rosalind Fernell was decidedly fat, as has been said before. She wore just now a one-piece dress of very brightly colored summer goods, with the figures so mixed up that Nancy remembered her brother Ted's calling this style "circus clothes."

Nancy, disregarding Rosalind's suggestion for a ribbon around her head to make up a dinner costume, had managed to slip into the simple white voile that her mother was so solicitous about having exactly on top of her bag, so that she could slip into it quickly, and this with the yellow ribbon band around her dark hair completed, rather than composed, the costume.

"You look perfectly duckie," declared Rosalind, giving her cousin a frankly admiring glance. "And I'm glad you did dress up, for maybe Gar will be over."

"Who's Gar?" asked Nancy.

"He's my—lifeguard; I'd perish without Garfield Durand. He lives on the next pile of rocks and he's more fun than a troop. You'll love Gar, I'm sure. There's Baldy calling dinner. Baldy is the butler, you know, and he's the most perfect baldy you ever gazed at. Has a head like the crystal ball in the back yard."

For a camp, which was really what this

summer home was supposed to be, Nancy thought everything about her most elaborate. The house was as heavily built as any city house might be, and the big beamed ceiling in the long dining room, made her think of an old English picture. The butler, Thomas, called Baldy, by the irrepressible Rosalind, rather awed Nancy at first, but, unlike the butlers in fiction, he could smile, and he could bend and he was human, so that after her chair had been adjusted and her water poured, Nancy presently felt quite at ease and enjoyed, rather than feared, her surroundings. Margot sat at Rosalind's side and Nancy was placed opposite. After all, she thought, one's simple meals at home were no different from that being served, except that at home things came more promptly and—yes—perhaps they did taste a little better mother's way. However, the soup was good and the chicken easy to eat, while the dessert was piled high with cream and Nancy ate it—to make her fat.

"Rosalind, you had better have—" Margot was objecting.

"Nop-ee, I'm going to have *this*," interrupted Rosalind, who took the overly rich dessert in defiance of ounces more of the much detested fat, which were bound to follow.

"Mrs. Fred phoned that she was detained in the city and so could not be here to greet you, Nancy," Margot said, as Thomas pulled out her chair, "but I'm sure Rosalind wants you all to herself, so Mrs. Fred need not be anxious." This little pleasantry was followed up by an effusive reply from Rosalind, who couldn't really seem to get close enough to Nancy for her own affectionate satisfaction.

"Oh, we'll be all right, Margot," she assured the tall woman with the unavoidable horn-rimmed glasses. "We've got oodles of things to talk about, and piles of things to do. You won't mind if I let up on the exercise to-night, will you?"

"But you know, Rosie—"

"'Course I do, Margy," and Rosalind coaxed prettily. But I want to entertain Cousin Nancy—"

The smiling assent from Margot seemed

unnecessary, for Rosalind was trooping off, with her arm around Nancy's waist, and her laughter bubbling like the soap-suds Ted loved to blow out of his old corn-cob pipe.

Nancy couldn't help thinking of her brother Ted, the boy now far away at camp, for, somehow, she was missing him in spite of all this strange adventure. He was always such a jolly little fellow. What a lark he would have had in this big place and how he would contrive to turn every little incident into a laugh or a chuckle? While Rosalind was speaking to the butler, and while she gave some message to Margot, Nancy had just a little time for ruminating. She wondered what her mother was doing. And how the long summer ahead would turn out for each of her small, intimate family.

"Come into my room," said Rosalind at her elbow, as they once again had mounted the broad stairs. "It's right next to yours—I thought you might be scary if I put you over in the guest room," said the cousin, considerately.

"I should much rather be near you, thanks Rosa," replied Nancy, meaning exactly what she said, for with real night settling down upon the mountains, a queer loneliness amounting almost to foreboding seemed to seize upon her.

"And you are never lonely out here?" she could not resist remarking, for it seemed to her Rosalind's spirits were mounting higher each moment. She laughed at the slightest excuse, and appeared to Nancy somewhat over excited.

"Well, of course, sometimes I have been. But not since Gar came. He was abroad last summer, but now—why, he drives me every place when Margot and Chet think I'm—doing something else."

This last piece of information was almost whispered to Nancy, and it was not difficult for her to guess that Rosalind indulged in pranks as well as in bubbling laughter.

"But you don't really go out without your daddy's knowing?" Nancy timidly asked.

"Bless the infant!" cooed Rosalind, "I do believe she's a regular little darling, country coz," and another demonstration accompanied that. "But I won't shock you to death. I'm really quite harmless, and you see," her face sobered for a moment, "all that I do concerns myself. I think I should have the privilege of enjoying myself, don't you?"

"Why, yes, of course. That is—" Already Nancy found herself perplexed. What if Rosalind was as risky as she pretended to be; and if she, Nancy, would find it difficult to keep free from responsibility?

"You know Orilla, she's the girl who used to live here, is too smart for words," imparted Rosalind, as the two girls delayed in Rosalind's beautiful golden room. "She believes she can help me to—to get thin" (there was wistfulness in this remark), "but Betty just can't bear her. So, of course, I have to do lots of things on the sly."

Instantly there flashed before Nancy's mind the suggestion her mother had made concerning this girl, Orilla. And a suspicious, jealous girl is not less dangerous just because she happens to be young. In fact, thought

Nancy, that would only make her less wise and more foolish.

CHAPTER IV

FROM THE NEXT PILE OF ROCKS

Grave misgivings flooded into Nancy's mind. She had known of Rosalind's peculiarities, had often heard her mother express keen regret that she, Uncle Frederic's own sister, could not have done something to supply the mother-need for Rosalind when Katherine Fernell was taken from her daughter.

And it seemed more unfortunate than otherwise, that Uncle Fred's position guaranteed so much hired care for Rosalind, because it was this fact that had separated her from Mrs. Brandon, Nancy's mother herself having been separated from her brother through a circumstance not unlike this very issue.

Not that Nancy bothered now to recall all this, but just because the "why" of her own circumstances compared oddly with the "why not" of Rosalind's. It appeared that Rosalind did not know why she should not "sneak off to ride with Gar" when she was supposed to be following all the rules of Fernlode, which must have forbidden this.

"I suppose it is not that I'm any better than Rosa," the puzzled Nancy was thinking, "but just because mother made me think differently."

"Nance, I suppose you are tired from that long, dirty train ride," suggested Rosalind, who was getting out a wrap for herself and another for Nancy. "Suppose we just scout around a little?"

"Scout around?"

"Yeppy. First let's make sure you're acquainted with your room, because you might want to come in before I do," said Rosalind. "Here's all the night stuff, but I don't suppose you try to bathe and scour off fat as I do. At any rate, do just as you please. Lock your door and yell through the keyhole at Margot, and if she asks for me—"

"Won't you be—in?"

"Oh, yes, of course," Rosalind hurried to

assure the puzzled girl. "I'm just preparing for emergencies. You see, I always expect them, but they somehow seldom come." A little sigh took years from Rosalind's heavy shoulders. She was acting now like such a very little girl, just sighing for romance and adventure.

On the big front porch, they tried the swing. As ever Rosalind cuddled up to Nancy in that eager, impulsive way that made Nancy feel sort of old. She, not being demonstrative herself, leaving that prerogative for the small brother Ted, could not at once get used to Rosalind's effusions.

"You see, Nance," bubbled Rosalind, "I'm going to do something won-der-ful!" This last word was dragged out like a tape line measuring thrills. "I waited until you came—you see, Orilla is really won-der-ful. She's the very smartest thing. And you see, Nancy, *you* can't realize the curse of being fat."

A peal of laughter from the amused Nancy checked this.

"You can't really mean it, Rosa," she said.

"Being fat isn't anything. You're just growing, and you won't always be so—so stout," the visitor assured her cousin, kindly.

"No, you just bet I won't, not if I know it," declared Rosa, who even then chewed a chocolate drop. "I'm going to get thin while the folks are in Europe. Wait until you see Betty, then you'll understand. She's just eel-ly, and she loves slippery clothes, the shimmery-shimmery kind. How could she ever own me as a step-daughter?" Again the catchy little sigh betrayed Rosa's state of mind. Nancy was beginning to wonder if she might not be a little bit jealous of the famously beautiful Betty.

"But don't you know," cautioned Nancy, feeling more and more like a grandmother giving advice, "it's awfully dangerous to—to take off fat too suddenly."

"Don't believe a word of it," declared Rosa. "I'd take a chance on reducing pounds per day if I knew how. You see," shifting the cushion and kicking the swing into action, "I inherit it from Grandmother Cashion, mother's mother. She was fat. I have her picture. And she had curly hair like mine, so of course I just had to be like her," argued the surprising girl.

"But you also got the curls," suggested Nancy, in genuine admiration.

"Which I don't want. Orilla says they make me look fatter, more babyish, you know."

"I suppose Orilla has thin hair," Nancy could not resist saying, for she was already convinced of Orilla's methods.

" 'Tis straightish, rather straggily," conceded Rosa. "But, you see, Orilla doesn't have to be pretty, she's so smart."

"What is she so smart about?" pressed Nancy.

"Oh, well, 'most everything," floundered Rosa. "She intends to be a nurse, no, a beauty doctor," she corrected herself. "That's why she's helping me."

"How's she doing it?" demanded Nancy, frankly.

"Oh, it's sort of a secret, but, of course, I'll

tell you later on," agreed Rosa.

"Does your—does Betty know?"

"Mercy me, no! She's the very last person on earth to know," said Rosa tragically. "I'm going to surprise her, and dad. It's all beautifully planned and I'm just waiting for them to sail, then I'll sail in."

"You're an awful lot like our Ted," Nancy told Rosa, a compliment unqualified.

"Is he fat?"

"A little. But I don't mean that way. I mean in making plans. He always has the most wonderful ideas—"

"I'd love Ted. What a shame you didn't bring him along."

"He would have been jolly," agreed the sister wistfully. "But you see, Ted needs to be trained. Being a boy without a father—"

"Just like me being a girl without a mother," spoke up Rosa. "I'd *love* to go to camp. In fact, father almost agreed, but Betty! You see Betty believes in white hands and slim ankles."

"Oh," said Nancy.

"Want to go around to the other side of the house? We can watch the boats from there. We have a motorboat but that's one thing dad is strict about. He just won't let me go on the water at night without him—imagine his having to be along always. And he won't let me go in a canoe even in broad daylight, unless I almost swear I'll stay in the cove, or just hug the edge. Dad is such a darling, I never would think of breaking my word to him," declared Rosa, her hand bruising Nancy's arm in making the declaration.

"We do feel that way when we love folks, don't we?" supplied Nancy. "Mother hardly asks me to promise anything, except where something might be dangerous, but it's fun to keep a promise as well as to break it, if you just think that way. I've a chum who spends most of her time planning to fool folks. Maybe I'm old fashioned, but I've tried it and it didn't turn out so funny. Once when I tried to fool Ted by locking him out, he just climbed in a window I couldn't reach, and I came pretty near having to stay out in the rain all night. You see, Miss Manners, we call her Manny—is to us about like Margot is to you. Except, of course, she isn't a servant, she's a dear friend we found last year out at Long Leigh. We had a great time last summer," Nancy continued. "I'll have to tell you about it some time."

"I'd love to hear. You had a shop or something, didn't you?"

"Yes, a funny little store we turned into almost everything but a church," laughed Nancy. They were moving around the winding porch and Nancy felt relieved that Rosa seemed to be more contented than she had been at dinner time. Surely she wasn't thinking of stealing off any place?

"Doesn't the lake look lovely with all the boats lighted up?" Rosa exclaimed. "With the big black mountains at the back and the little firefly boats in front—I guess this is one of the most beautiful lakes in America," she finished.

"It is glorious," agreed Nancy. "But it makes me feel sort of awe-stricken," she admitted.

"Not homesick? That isn't just a nice way of saying you're homesick, Nance?" asked Rosa solicitously.

"Oh, no indeed, Rosa," denied Nancy. "But I was just thinking how dark it can be under all these trees."

"And this house hasn't a bright spot in it," added Rosa. "I wonder why folks build with black beams in forests? And they always seem to. If I were planning a mountain camp I'd have white pine wood and turn yellow paint on with a hose, inside and out," she declared. A car was coming up the winding drive, its headlights threading their way through the trees in glaring billows.

"There's Gar!" exclaimed Rosa, joy juggling the words. "I'm so glad he came over! Now, you won't be homesick."

"I wasn't," defended Nancy. But the car was at the steps now and Rosa was racing off in that direction. The prospect of meeting a strange boy fluttered Nancy, naturally, but perhaps she would have been more self-conscious had the caller been a girl. Girls are supposed to be critical, and Nancy's wardrobe was not elaborate, but boys—well boys ought to be jolly. She knew that Ted and his little friends would still be when they grew up.

"My cousin, you know, Gar," Rosa was exclaiming, as the youth in white knickers, with his prep school sweater of violent yellow, came along the porch.

The introductions over, Nancy knew she was going to like Garfield Durand. His manner toward Rosa was that of a big brother, and he did not hesitate to argue against many of her suggestions.

"Can't take you out, Rosa, unless you're sure your dad won't mind," he said frankly. Then turning to Nancy, "Don't *you* think it's silly to be meeting that Orilla girl—"

"Gar!" came Rosa's warning. "Please don't tell *all* my secrets at once. I'm sorry if I bother you—"

"Oh, now Rose, you know well enough I don't mean that," interrupted Gar. "It's just that you're so—so easy with Orilla, and she's a fox, only you won't believe it," declared the boy, flushing.

An awkward silence followed that remark. It was very plain that Rosa objected to discussing Orilla and her ways before Nancy. It was also quite plain that the boy was trying to avoid something, perhaps a clandestined ride which Rosa seemed bent upon. He didn't settle himself down as one does who might expect to stay awhile; in fact, he first sat upon the porch rail, next straddled a bench, then flung himself into a rocker and seemed to find it impossible to obtain any position suitable to his turbulent mood.

"It's certainly early enough *now* to take a drive," suggested Rosa, pointedly.

"Oh, surely," agreed Gar. "Can't I take you and your cousin over to the Point, or some place?"

"Like a dear," replied Rosa. "I'll run and break the news to Margot. She still believes in you, Gar," and then Nancy found herself chatting to the boy, free from the unpleasant little discussion and at ease, because he seemed so frankly boyish and so eager to take her for the proposed drive.

"Don't mind my scrapping with Rose," he remarked. "She's such a kid and so easily influenced. And you see, Mr. Fernell trusts our folks to sort of keep track of her."

"Of course. That's splendid," agreed Nancy. "You see I'm sort of a stranger myself, and I guess Rosalind has been a lot alone—"

"You're the very thing for her, and maybe just in time," he said under his breath, with an intention by no means clear to Nancy.

"Just in time!" she thought. "Whatever can that mean?"

CHAPTER V

THE FALL IN THE WOODS

"We'll probably pick up Dell," suggested Garfield, referring to his sister who was found on the "next pile of rocks," as Rosa had described the Durand estate. She was older than her brother, much older than Rosa, and somehow this fact brought relief to Nancy, who was fearing things she couldn't quite define. It seemed safer, however, to have an older girl along, and when Dell Durand jumped into the car and added her part to the fun of driving through the woods, up and down hills, in and out of sly curves that often brought Nancy's breath up sharply, she talked to Nancy in the sensible, intelligent way that she, Nancy, was most accustomed to.

"We couldn't live up here if it were not for the fun at the Point," Dell declared. "It's all well enough in the daytime—plenty of sport then for anyone who likes the water, mountains or—pet dogs," she said this sarcastically, "but if we didn't have the pavilion for dancing and the movies and such things, I'm afraid we would find the evenings—long!"

"Shall we go over to Bent's?" called Gar from the wheel.

"Just as Rosa says," replied his sister politely.

"I'm afraid Nancy may be tired," replied Rosa considerately. "I haven't given her a minute since she landed, and you know what that Boston and Maine train does to you. No—guess we'll just peek in at the pavilion. I'm afraid I couldn't sleep a wink if I didn't get a little something to pep me up," sighed Rosa. "That house with Margot and Thomas can get on—one's—nerves—"

"Nerves!" mocked Gar. "Say, Rosie, when you get nerves I'll get—"

"Sense," supplied Rosa, imitating the boy's voice. "Anyhow I have a little of that—"

"Quit your squabbling, babes," ordered Dell. "Can't you behave before company?"

Just then the pavilion loomed up, with the paper covered lights and jazzing music, not the usual, ordinary summer place, but rather a little spot in the wilderness where, evidently, the young folks of Craggy Bluff found such evening entertainment as Dell had so briefly described.

It was all a little strange to Nancy, who had never before been thrown in with such grown up young folks. Even Rosa, although in reality only a few months older than Nancy, seemed very grown up and superficial, now that she was mingling with numbers of friends who promptly greeted their arrival at the dance hall.

Gar took himself and his car off, excusing himself to join other boys who claimed him, while Rosa insisted upon Nancy dancing.

"Let's wait a while," Nancy coaxed, not wishing to lose herself at once in the gliding dancers.

"Can't," objected Rosa. "I've got to dance. It's good for me," she whispered; and when the two girls did glide off, Nancy was agreeably surprised at the ease displayed by her cousin.

"Just like floating," Rosa explained. "I can float all day. And dancing is such a silly walk, isn't it? Don't even have to bend."

It was not much more than a rhythmic walk, and as for bending—surely that was quite out of question, for that season's dance was markedly a glide.

Dell was dancing with some young man, and Gar was not to be seen about, when Rosa led Nancy over to a corner of the platform.

"I just thought I saw—someone I knew over here," she said, "Orilla, you know. But I don't imagine she would be out here—she's so busy, always."

Rosa was peering into the dark corners where some few persons stood watching the dancers. Somehow Nancy was secretly hoping that Rosa was mistaken, for while she had a certain curiosity to see this much talked of Orilla, she would rather have delayed the experience until some other time.

"I guess it wasn't she," Rosa said finally,

still jerking her head from side to side attempting to find the face she was seeking for. "Yes," she exclaimed again, "I do believe I see her. Glide over this way—"

"Isn't it too dark along the edge?" Nancy asked. She did not like the idea of getting so far away from Dell. Besides that, it really was dark and deserted at that end of the platform.

But Rosa was bent upon following the figure she either saw or imagined she saw. In fact, so intent was she, that Nancy's remark went by unnoticed.

"Wait here just a minute," Rosa said suddenly, dropping Nancy's arm and dashing off along the uncertain edge of the circular platform.

Fear seized Nancy! What if Rosa was as foolish as Garfield had hinted, and what if she should run off even for a short time on some silly pretext with the undesirable Orilla? Gar had said that Nancy had arrived "just in time." What could he have meant?

She was watching Rosa's light dress and

felt she would surely have to follow her. No matter what Rosa had said about Nancy waiting, she was going to keep as close—

The flash of Rosa's dress had gone out like a candle flame in the wind. Turning her own steps in the direction Rosa must have taken, she hurried along the platform's edge and just caught a glimmer of something light—Rosa's dress it must have been—darting through the trees, away from the pavilion.

"Rosalind!" she called anxiously. "Rosa!"

A queer little twittering whistle, that could not have been an answer from Rosalind, pierced the darkness. The music had ceased, that dance was over and now the young folks were all flocking in the other direction. Nancy saw this, too, as she stepped off the platform and attempted to follow the hidden trail of Rosalind.

"How absurd!" she could not help sighing, "if this is the way I'm going to spend my summer chasing after a foolish girl—"

The next moment she was sure she heard whispering. That certainly was Rosa, but why should she be hiding?

"Rosa!" again called Nancy, this time feeling very much like turning back to Dell and leaving Rosa to report for herself.

Indignant and offended, Nancy was almost about to follow out that thought when a sudden sharp cry—it was from Rosa—certainly—a cry of pain came from a spot close by.

"Oh, Orilla! quick!" Nancy heard. "My foot is caught and—"

"Rosa, where are you?" sharply demanded Nancy. "*I'm* here! I can help you!"

"She's all right—" came a voice not Rosa's. Then the flash of a small light betrayed the spot where Rosa had fallen.

"It's my foot, it got caught in briars, and oh, mercy!" Rosa exclaimed, "I'm afraid I've sprained my ankle!"

By this time Nancy could see Rosa's companion. So that was Orilla! A tall girl with fiery red hair that even in the glimmering light of the hand flash which she, Orilla, was holding, looked too red to be pretty. It was as if the head that held it all was in a real blaze, rather than being covered with hair.

"Oh, you're all right, Rose. Get up," the girl ordered so unkindly that Nancy bent over and put her arm about the struggling figure.

"Did you ever see anything—so—so—beastly!" poor Rose was muttering. "Just to jump into a hole and get strangled with briars—"

"Hold on to me, dear." Nancy could not help offering the endearing term, for the red-haired girl surely was scoffing. And Rosa's every attempt to seem grown up, her foolish little expressions, and her disregard of that sort of conduct which Nancy very well knew was Rosa's natural manner just being held back, made the cousin all the more an object of affection to Nancy. She was now Rosa's champion against this girl, Orilla.

"Showing off," was what it all was, of course, but there was something more important to think of just now. Rosa was hurt, the Durands were not in sight and Nancy was simply frightened to death at the whole situation.

"Can't you really get up?" asked Orilla, showing some concern herself now. She was holding the flash light over Rosa, and in the darkness its rays shone clear and remarkably bright for a thing so small. It picked out a mass of wicked briars and treacherous undergrowth into which Rosa had fallen.

"I can't—stir—" she moaned. "There's a regular rope of something around—my—leg. Oh-h-h!"

It was not hard to realize that a rope of something had indeed imprisoned the girl, for even the efforts of Orilla joining those of Nancy, failed to extricate the injured one.

"What—shall—we do!" breathed Nancy, more deeply concerned than she wished to admit even to herself. "However will we get her out of this?"

"Silly thing for her to get into," grumbled the red-haired girl. "But I guess I can chop her out."

"Chop her out!" exclaimed Nancy, incredulously.

"Yes. I've got tools. You stay here with

her, and for goodness' sake keep her quiet. My car is over on the road. I'll be back as quickly as I can get here."

Presently the two girls found themselves alone, in the dark, in that lonesome wood. Nancy was too frightened to do more than keep whispering courage to Rosa, and Rosa was too miserable to do more than groan.

"Why—" started Nancy once more, but checked the query before it was formed. Of what use to question Rosa now? The thing to do was to hope for Orilla's return. But even that worried Nancy.

"Oh, Nance," groaned Rosa, "if my poor leg is broken—"

"It isn't, dear, I'm sure," consoled Nancy. "You know a strain feels dreadfully at first. Are you sure she'll come back?"

"Oh, yes. She sounds mean, but that's her way," Rosa explained. "Can't you see her light? Isn't she coming yet?"

"No," replied Nancy. "And Rosa, I feel I'll just have to go back to the pavilion for Dell. What will they think?"

"Think we're lost, maybe." Rosa was tugging at the briars and uttering groans at every attempt to free herself. Nancy had torn the skin from her right hand in her attempts to help, but was still working carefully.

"How far is the road?" Nancy asked presently.

"Just there, behind that little hill. You can't see it, of course—"

"Will you stay while I look for Dell?"

"I'll have to. But oh, Nance," as her cousin prepared to go, "you know I don't want them to see me meeting Orilla. They just wouldn't understand. Every one hates her so and she's so bitter about it. Look again. Isn't she coming?"

Mystified, Nancy obeyed.

"Yes, I believe she is. There's a spark—yes, it's her light," she added relievedly. "But how will she chop you out?"

"She carries tools; she'll have a little chopper—a small ax, you know," faltered Rosa, relief showing also in her voice.

"You mean a hatchet. Why would she carry a hatchet?"

"Oh, I'll tell you, sometime; if I ever get out of this," groaned Rosa, digging her fingers deep into the flesh of Nancy's arm to which she was clinging.

The faithful little flash-light dispelled what darkness it could reach, as the girl with the small hatchet hurried back to them.

"Now don't move while I chop," she ordered sharply. "I'm hours late now, and I've got to hurry."

"Being late—" began Nancy indignantly. But holding back the briars and bushes while Orilla chopped at that which so securely bound Rosa, precluded anything like objections to the apparent heartlessness of Orilla.

"There; I guess you can get up now. Hope to goodness I'm not all stung with poison-ivy," Orilla snarled, while Nancy gave her entire attention to the unfortunate cousin.

"Put your arm under her other arm," she ordered Orilla. "Her ankle is hurt, you know," she finished sarcastically.

"Oh yes, I know," sneered the red-haired one. But nevertheless she did as Nancy Brandon ordered her to do.

CHAPTER VI

A STRANGE RESCUE

Although both Nancy and Orilla gave all their strength to the task, it was only with great difficulty that they succeeded in getting poor Rosa over to the pavilion.

"Now try," insisted Orilla for times repeated, "not to attract attention. It's awful to be always getting in scrapes—"

"Orilla Rigney! You just hush!" spoke up Rosa quite unexpectedly. "You make me sick. One would think I did this purposely, when I was merely following—"

"Land sakes, you hush!" begged Orilla, her tone of voice changing instantly from that of the arrogant boss to that of the humble petitioner. "I know it was an accident."

"Oh, do you? Nice of you, I'm sure. I guess I know it—ouch!" A necessarily sudden move took all the courage from Rosa. She sank down upon the edge of the platform, her arms actually clutching at Nancy's knees.

"Well, you don't have to be such a baby," snapped Orilla.

"Better a baby than a fool," quarreled Rosa.

"Please don't excite yourself, Rosa," begged Nancy. "The thing to do now—"

"Oh, let her talk," sneered Orilla. "That's the best thing she can do—"

"But I won't let *you* talk in that voice without—without talking back," spoke up Nancy. "At least you are old enough to have sense—"

"If I were able I'd love this three-cornered fight," put in Rosa, attempting to prevent that very thing. "But as it is—well, I can see myself in dry-dock all summer."

"For a scratched ankle!" again sneered Orilla.

But Nancy had made up her mind. They were now safe upon the lighted platform, and she was going at once to find Dell, and she hoped Gar would be with her. Scarcely waiting to explain this to Rosa—Orilla she could not help ignoring—she hurried off.

"But do hurry back, Nancy," begged Rosa, whose face could now be seen and it showed her suffering. "I'm nearly dead—"

"Don't be such a baby," Nancy again heard Orilla mutter, just as she hurried off.

Dancers impeded her way, and she was obliged to do some skillful dodging in and out of the movements to avoid actual collision. But Nancy scarcely saw them. Neither did she hear the jolly music, for it seemed to her tragic that such an accident should befall Rosa. It was only human for Nancy to feel impending gloom, so far as her vacation was concerned, but her dislike for Orilla, and the little mother instinct that so spontaneously went forth to save Rosa, had more to do with her thoughts than any possible loss of good times.

"I guess I've got something to do," she was telling herself as she peered into face after face, hoping to pick out that of Dell or Gar Durand.

"Looking for us, too, I suppose," she sighed. Then, realizing that they must know Rosa and her habits better than she did, came the discouraging fear that they too might be off in the woods—hunting for Rosa.

Moments seemed like hours, and every time Nancy espied someone who looked a little bit like Dell and presently found she was mistaken, her resources would wane.

"If it had been any other time," she couldn't help grumbling, "when I knew persons and places. But the very first night—"

"Woo-hoo!" came a call. Then: "Nan-cee!"

"Oh, there she is!" cried Nancy aloud, disregarding those around her. "Dell!" she called. "Here I am!"

In a moment Dell, her own face showing relief at the locating of Nancy, sprang up to her side and just grabbed her.

"You runaway! Where ever have you been?"

"Oh Dell, do hurry!" whispered Nancy. "Where is your brother?"

"Child! What is it?"

"Rosa's hurt." The words were driven straight into Dell's anxious ears.

"Rosa—"

"Hush," warned Nancy. "Can you get your brother?"

"Yes. He started at the other end. Don't leave this spot. See, it's the big post—" and Dell was off to locate her brother.

Briefly, very briefly, Nancy attempted to give Dell and Garfield some account of Rosa's troubles, as presently they were all hurrying toward the sequestered spot where Rosa waited. She did not mention Orilla—somchow she felt that Rosa would not have wanted her to. Better let her cousin explain that angle, Nancy wisely decided.

But before they had actually come up to Rosa, Nancy saw that she was alone: that Orilla had left her!

"Oh, you poor darling!" exclaimed Dell with genuine sympathy. "To think you were here all alone, and we were hunting—"

"Slipped off into the rocks," said Rosa simply, "and not even a life-guard around. Gar, how are you going to tow me in?"

"How come?" asked the boy. "Something 'busted', really?"

"A leg or two," replied Rosa, "and it hurts like thunder, if you must know the horrible details. Give me a lift. Margot will have the fire department out—"

"Wait till I get the car. There's a lane along here—"

"Trust Gar to know the lanes," said Rosa, her spirits soaring with the presence of her friends.

In snatches she and Nancy told Dell something of what had happened—just something. It did not seem necessary to speak of Orilla, although there was a gap in her story when Rosa insisted she had simply been bound by ropes of briars and couldn't possibly break loose. It was taken for granted then that she did eventually, somehow, "break loose", and the actual "chopping out" was thus entirely omitted from the recital.

A welcome little toot from the horn of Gar's car told them that he had made his way through the lane, and the next moment he was again upon the platform, planning how best to get Rosa into the car.

No one joked about her size, nor did they blame her for the predicament, for it was rather a serious matter, as each understood it, and only Rosa herself was privileged to do any joking.

"I can limp if you'll promise me not to let me step for a single step on that game ankle," she told her friends. "I never knew *one* ankle could hurt as badly as this does."

Gar and Dell insisted upon doing the lifting, as they really were much stronger than Nancy, so with the car lights to guide them, they practically carried Rosa through the little patch that separated the pavilion from the roadway.

Even so, the journey was not accomplished without groans, grunts and admonitions, and it was growing more clear to Nancy each moment that the fat cousin was really quite a baby after all.

She wondered what had become of Orilla. It seemed improbable she should have entirely deserted the injured girl, and as the car was cautiously backed out into the clearance,

Nancy kept watching for little flashes of the light which Orilla had carried.

Deeper resentment bore down upon her, however, as they finally made the main road without a single flash sending forth a secret farewell signal.

"How can Rosa be so indifferent to such treatment?" Nancy kept asking herself. "And why ever does she bother with that girl?"

Meanwhile Gar, from his place at the wheel, could be heard questioning Rosa. She was sitting in front because that position was deemed the easiest riding, and now, as they all sped off toward Fernlode, some of the terrors of the accident seemed lifted.

"No fooling now, Rosa," Gar was saying, "how did that happen? *You* can't fool me—"

"Gar Durand! How does a broken leg ever happen? It just breaks, doesn't it?" evaded Rosa.

"Not just like that, it doesn't. It has to *get* broken, and I'll bet a peanut you were up to something—"

"The dopy-doc has got to fix you up, Rosa, you know," interrupted Dell. "Perhaps we had better pick him up or give him a call on our way out. You know what a fuss he makes about night visits."

"Margot would simply pass away and we'd have a double funeral, if we brought the dopy-doc up to the house, bodily," replied Rosa. "Not that I want him a—tall—"

"Better get him," insisted Gar. "I can't keep lugging you around—"

"As if I'd *let* you!" Rosa parried.

"If you keep on getting better this way, Rosa," put in Nancy, "I don't believe you'll need any doctor."

"Bright idea! Wonderful coz! I don't want the dopy-doc," exclaimed Rosa. "Why should I have him until—"

"We are sure," drawled Gar, "that the injuries are fatal."

"Fatal?" repeated his sister. "You mean serious."

"No, I don't either. I mean—"

"Ouch!" yelled Rosa. "There you all go;

mocking me. That's the worst it has hurt—yet—"

Which turn of affairs fully decided Dell, for she gave definite orders then that Gar should stop for Doctor Easton, loquaciously called by Rosa, the dopy-doc.

"I'll tell him to come out tonight," she declared in the face of Rosa's pleas and protests. "Can't tell what a game ankle may do, and while I'm in charge—"

"You're perfectly right," insisted Nancy under her breath, rejoicing that someone would take Rosa in actual charge.

"And we'll all be so late—" grumbled Gar, in that good-natured way boys have, "that our family will have the megaphone out. Nancy," he said politely, remembering that she was, after all, something of a stranger, "whenever you hear the megaphone you'll know there is nothing the matter. It's mother's warning to be careful of the water."

"Now watch Margot take a fit when she sees you help me—please don't call Baldy, Dell, he uses hair-oil," said Rosa, when the car was pulled up in front of the side porch and the girls with Gar were promptly alighting, "and he's sure to sling me over his shoulder, if he gets the chance."

The next half hour was consumed in getting Rosa installed in her bed and "fussed up", as Nancy put it, and also in the appeasing of Margot, who would not be satisfied with the account of the accident.

"Turned on her ankle!" insisted Dell.

"Turned on her ankle," reiterated Gar, who just "hung around" waiting for the doctor.

"Really, I can't see—" moaned the distressed woman.

"But it's only her ankle," chanted Nancy.

"Say Maggie," sang out Rosalind, from her billowy pillows, "do you want me to have something else the matter? Because if you do I can exhibit a wonderful array of scratches—"

"The doctor," announced Margot, solemnly.

"The doctor," repeated Rosalind, comically.

"The dopy-doc," whispered Dell. "Let you and me escape, Nan," she suggested.

CHAPTER VII

LOVELY LADY BETTY

It seems the ankle was not sprained after all. Rosa spent one day trying on all her sick-spell caps, the little gifts she had not yet had a chance to wear, trying on her fancy silk robes—there was that beauty, Betty had brought her from Paris, it was glorious and she had never really worn it before.

Nancy never before had seen such beautiful things, and Rosa insisted that she too try some of them on. It was in this way the cousin tactfully bestowed upon Nancy a lot of pretty things "just presents I should have sent on Christmas and on birthdays," insisted Rosa.

"But wait until Dad and Betty come," threatened Rosa. "They'll want me all put in splints, see if they don't. Betty seems to think I'll melt, like gelatine, if I'm left out of the ice-box," she finished, a little bitterly.

"Now, Rosa," objected Nancy, "maybe you're not fair. I can guess that Betty feels like your mother, even if she isn't, and that would make her worry a lot more about you. Since I've been away from my mother I know what a lot of things she has been doing for me, in spite of keeping up her library business. My clothes seem to be all upset already—"

"Give them to Margot, she adores fixing clothes," interrupted Rosa, losing the point Nancy had tried to make regarding the pretty step-mother. "I honestly do believe she musses my things up just for the joy of straightening them out again."

"How funny! But I don't really mean that I can't look after my things, Rosa," explained Nancy, "although I did use to think no girl in the world could hate such work more than I did—"

"I don't mind it a bit," interrupted Rosa grandly. "I often wash out laces and my fine stockings—"

"Oh," said Nancy with one of her twisted

smiles, "I don't mind just that, either. But Rosa, hadn't you better get off that foot? You've been standing on it for almost half an hour."

"Just as you say, Coz," agreed Rosa, who did seem strangely willing to agree with most of Nancy's suggestions. "You don't know what this ankle means to me. I haven't told you—"

"What?" asked Nancy, bluntly.

"Oh, something—great!" and the baby blue eyes fairly whirled around in Rosa's face as she turned them up, down, from right to left and then the other way, expressing the wonderment she had so vaguely hinted at.

"Think you might tell me," teased Nancy. In fact the big secret between Rosa and Orilla was growing more and more mystifying to the visitor.

"I do intend to tell you, of course, Nancy," confided Rosa, her face falling into the rarely serious lines which this subject could provoke. "But not just—yet." She drawled these last words intentionally and the refusal to answer her question piqued Nancy. In fact, she dropped Rosa's prettiest scarf down in a heap without even pretending to fold it.

"Mad?" teased Rosa.

"No, of course not. But Rosa, it is queer, the way you act about that girl." She just couldn't say Orilla.

"Nan-cee." Rosa had both her arms around the pouting cousin. "You're not jealous! You see—oh, you see I haven't had any body else; not anybody, and Orilla has been kind to me—"

"Even Gar doesn't like her," flung back Nancy.

"No, that's so. He hates her. But then you see, I've been an awful nuisance to Gar on account of it all."

"How—a nuisance?"

"Nancy Brandon, you're what my dad calls an idealist!" exclaimed Rosa, bubbling back into her usual jolly mood. "Know what that is? I've looked it up for it's dad's pet word. It means one who—"

"Ideals I suppose," said Nancy, herself

recovering the good humored mood. "Well, never mind, Rosa. Just so long as you don't run away any more, or break any more ankles, I won't mind," and she wound the lately despised scarf around Rosa's plump shoulders, with great affectation.

It was turning out to be a rainy day, so that the girls' enforced idleness was not a real hardship. They were having a splendid time, especially Nancy, who, being just a normal girl, delighted in seeing beautiful clothes. And Rosa did have them—stacks of them. Not only was she the possessor of gowns by the dozen, but the finest of silk underthings, some of them so cob-webby that Nancy frankly questioned their utility.

"Please don't give me anything else, Rosa," she pleaded. "I shan't know what to do with such finery."

"Don't worry, love," replied Rosa. "Nobody knows exactly what to do with them until they've been worn a time or two. That's dad's joke about the man's boots, you know. He couldn't get them on until after he had worn them a time or two!"

"Pretty good!" agreed Nancy. "I'll remember that. But Rosa—oh, here comes the car!"

"With Betty and dad. Let me get into bed. I must look sick enough to ward off a scolding!"

She dropped such bits of clothing as she had been draping herself in, and scuttled into bed. Nancy felt quite nervous enough at the prospect of meeting the pretty Lady Betty, but with Rosa's condition to be explained, the home-coming seemed rather exciting.

Margot rushed into the bedroom. "Your father is coming, my dear child," she pronounced, "and Mrs. Betty. Now please don't get them all worried and anxious—" she paused as she patted the innumerable pillows.

"Get them worried! Indeed! And my poor foot—Hello, Daddy!" called out Rosalind. "My leg's broke!"

The bombastic greeting was taken up by her daddy who promptly and lustily shouted:

"Hello, Rosalinda! Which leg?"

Proudly Rosa stuck the injured member, in its white bandages, outside the bed covering.

"That one! 'Busted' badly!" She mocked. "But Daddy, there's Nancy. She's scared to death of me, Nancy, come over here—"

Nancy knew Rosa's father, the handsome Uncle Frederic who had visited them in their own little home, so she was not at all embarrassed in greeting him.

He was as tall and handsome as ever, Nancy could not help noticing, and his welcome to her made her feel almost comfortable—if only she had the meeting of his new wife over with.

"Where's Betty?" asked Rosa, rather quietly when her father had taken his place beside her bed.

"She'll be along presently. We had rather a tiring drive—the roads are in their usual bad summer condition. But tell me about the accident, Linda? How did it all happen?"

As father and daughter talked, Nancy noticed how particular he was to know as much and more than Rosa seemed anxious to tell.

He was most solicitous about Rosa's condition, however, and so affectionate that he called her a different name each time he addressed her, yet he was very positive in his manner. Evidently, he was not too sure of his daughter's prudence.

"Of course, it's all right for you to go out to the park with Garfield and Adell," he said, "but never alone, Rosy-kins, not even with Nancy and in the day-time. Remember, I don't want to have you lost in the New Hampshire forests, you know."

Rosa fairly glowed under her father's interest and affection. Sitting by the window and watching this play, Nancy realized what Rosa's father meant to her—just what Nancy's mother meant to Nancy.

"We don't know until we are away from it," she reasoned, choking back the wave of home-sickness that threatened to creep over her. "I don't see why Rosa thinks she is left out of everything; that she is too fat to be happy," went on Nancy's deliberation. "Her father just idolizes her."

A little flutter from the doorway seemed to answer that, for presently the lovely Betty—Lady Betty, as Nancy was privately calling the new aunt, appeared before them.

She *was* lovely; Nancy conceded that instantly, and surrounding her, like a halo of loveliness, was a faint something which recalled to Nancy the perfection of Miss Manners' hand-made laces—a combination of inspiration and perfectly chosen materials. No wonder her Uncle Frederic had been fascinated by Betty Burnett. Surely she was lovely.

"Sweet-heart!" she almost sang to Rosalind. "What has happened to you? Don't tell me—"

"Busted me leg!" sang back Rosa, impishly. "But, Betty dear, there's Nancy. You are going to love her because she—is skinny!"

The next few moments were lost to Nancy in her confusing introduction. Betty was being kind, kind to the point of gush, Nancy feared, but then Rosa had been absurdly blunt and so had sort of challenged their meeting. The explosion of slang betrayed

Rosa's own feelings. She was insisting that Betty would love a thin girl and intimating broadly that she hated fat ones.

While all this was going on, and especially a little later when Uncle Frederic had arranged his wife's blue cushions in the big blue bird chair (Betty was, of course, a dainty blonde), Nancy found her eyes devouring the picture.

This was the wonderful, the beautiful Betty who had taken—so Rosa said—Rosa's place in the tall iron-gray man's heart. Who had put Orilla out of what she had been brought up to consider her home, and worst of all, if true, it was she who had brought unhappiness to little Rosa, because her own flawless beauty was contrasting so painfully with the ungraceful lines of Rosalind Fernell.

It must be remembered that Nancy Brandon was a girl whose home influence was almost opposite that of Rosa's. Her mother and brother Ted were dear, darling chums, all and each a part of the other's existence. Also, that Nancy's mother was employed in a public library, so that books had become a real part of Nancy's life. And books are very good friends indeed. They almost always try to make folks more tolerant and more reasonable with their surroundings and companions.

But here was Rosa, a girl who only read books when she had to, or when Margot threatened her with something worse to do. She had had little chance to learn the simple things that stood for so much in Nancy's life, and while Nancy could not have reasoned this way, it is only fair to understand Rosa and her peculiar self-made troubles.

Lady Betty was not exerting herself very much, in spite of Rosa's predicament. There had been the tiring drive, as Uncle Frederic had explained, and there was the sea-going voyage to-morrow—as everybody knew.

And Nancy was glad they were going away. Rosa had been positively rebellious ever since the pretty Betty had come into her room. Was it sheer nervousness? Nancy wondered. How perfectly silly for Rosa to keep sticking that bandaged foot outside the lace-edged sheet. And how absurd for her to keep using such senseless slang! Calling it a "busted foot" and insisting that she was "laid up for repairs"—it sounded like pure affectation to Nancy, who, while being no prude, was not a rebel, either.

CHAPTER VIII

ROSALIND'S SORROWS

During the half hour that Lady Betty favored them with her presence, no mention was made of Orilla. It was all a jumbling talk of what to get Rosa in Europe, and what Rosa should do while they were away.

"You see, Nancy dear," said Mrs. Betty. "I left my little pet Pompsie—"

"Her dog," interrupted Rosa.

"Rosa-linda!" exclaimed her father, rebukingly.

"Well, how would Nancy know—"

"I left my little dog with my sister, because Rosa might forget and lock him out on the roof some night. He adores to play on the roof—"

Then Margot appeared with a very small silver tray. It held a card which she handed to Lady Betty.

"Oh, dear!" she sighed. "Fred, there's the Prestons. Suppose you go down, like a love, while I slip into something. Rosa and Nancy be good girls. Nancy, your name is a hymn to me, it was also my grandmother's. She was a cameo lady, beautiful beyond words."

"No relation to our Nancy, then," again spoke the impish Rosa.

Both girls were brazenly glad when their elders were gone, and in spite of Margot's unwelcome ministrations, Rosa hopped out of bed, pushed Margot outside, shut the door, turned the key and undertook to execute an original dance, sort of "skippity-hop-to-the-barber-shop" fashion.

"Now you see, you see," she paused to tell Nancy, "just what I'm up—against!"

"Rosalind Fernell!" exclaimed Nancy. "Do you know you are just too silly for anything?"

"Maybe I am." The girl with the flying scarf came to a very abrupt stop and seemed to confront Nancy. "But I just want to tell you I can't love Betty. She's too dollified. Makes me feel like a—like a clown." The voice, usually so flippant, had suddenly become almost tragic. "And that's why, Nancy Brandon," continued the indignant Rosa, "I'm going to become less—clownish!"

"Rosa!"

Tears, tears unmistakable had gathered in the soft blue eyes, and Nancy was panic stricken at their appearance. She couldn't bear to cry herself, and she hated even worse than that to see any one else cry. And now, here was Rosa on the verge!

"I've just got to have it out!" moaned Rosa, dropping down again into her pillows. "Every time I see her I feel just the same. Oh, why couldn't daddy be satisfied with me? We were such—such—chums—"

Nancy felt too much like agreeing with this to offer any sensible advice, but she felt called upon to try.

"I'm sure she loves you, Rosa. You just think she's selfish—"

"Don't—go—preaching. I just hate it, Nancy. And I've got an awful—temper."

"So have I," calmly replied Nancy.

This brought Rosa's tear-stained face up from the pillows.

"Have you—honestly? That's because we're real cousins. Of course, Betty isn't any real relation to me." Rosa seemed very glad of that.

"Guess we are something alike," persisted Nancy, glad to change the subject. "We've both got—big—mouths—"

This was too much for Rosa. She simply roared, shouted, laughing, as so often a tiny child will, in the very face of its own tears.

"Big mouths!" she repeated. "Haven't we, though? Big, long, square mouths like, like prize fighters."

"No," objected Nancy, "like Abraham Lincoln's—"

This precipitated another gale of laughter, and only the insistent knocking, known to be Margot's, for her voice accompanied the demand, brought the two girls back from their gleeful frolic.

"You are coming down to dinner," ordered Margot, trying to make sure that her command would be obeyed.

"I certainly am *not*," fired back Rosa.

"But why? You can walk. I even heard you dance—"

"You ought to *see* me dance, Margot," answered the irrepressible Rosa. "Hearing me, isn't the half of it. Seeing me is well worth while. But, Margot," down dropped Rosa's tone to one of entreaty, "you be a lamb, and fix up a gor-gee-ous tray for me and Nancy. Just this once, Margot. You know how I feel—"

"Rosalind, I'm honestly afraid that Mrs. Fernell will blame me for your conduct." Margot drew her lips into so straight a line they didn't look like lips at all.

"Do come down, Rosa," pleaded Nancy, feeling very uncomfortable because of this willful girl's obstinacy. It was bad enough to be away from home, but to have to keep up this battle seemed unreasonable to Nancy.

"Not to-night. Please don't any one ask me," and again tears threatened Rosa's eyes. "If you don't want to bother with my tray,

Margot, just ask Baldy when he has time. There's—no—hurry—"

This appeal brought about the result plainly desired by Rosa, for not only did Margot agree to the request, but she went much further. She wrote out the dinner menu, and from this list of fine food Rosa made her selection, first politely consulting Nancy's taste.

"We live so differently," explained Nancy, who was now losing much of the natural timidity following her introduction into this home. "You see, we don't even keep a maid—"

"Oh, how jolly!" declared Rosa. "They're a set of spies."

"You don't mean that, Rosa," defended Nancy. "Why should a girl, who happens to be a maid, in any way be inferior—"

"Because she's a maid," insisted Rosa.

"But if you had to work, for instance, what would you be?"

"I'd run a beauty parlor," declared Rosa, thus betraying anxiety concerning her own personal appearance. "What would you do?" she countered.

"Well," Nancy hesitated, "you know I've always declared I hated housework. In fact, I suppose I don't really love it now, but last summer we had a cooking class at our little cottage, and really, Rosa, you have no idea how much fun there is in learning things with a lot of jolly girls."

"I'd rather boys," said contrary Rosa, "I'd like to learn to chop down trees and load guns and fish—"

"Yes, of course," agreed Nancy, "but, you see, I knew all that. Ted and I are regular campers-out, and we've done almost everything woodsy. Mother loves it too, so we've spent more time on hikes and in camps than we ever have under civilized roofs."

"You lucky dogs!" broke out Rosa, "I can't imagine having a mother who could actually stay out of doors all night."

"Oh, yes. Mother's a real sport," declared Nancy proudly. "But I doubt if you would like hiking and camping, Rosa. It's terribly hard on—on beauty," she faltered.

"Good for it! The best thing in the world.

It's this soft living that is making such a fluffy, fat caterpillar out of me."

"But caterpillars turn to butterflies—"

"Don't I know it? That's why, Nancy," hinted Rosa very mysteriously. "That's exactly—why!"

"Why what?" demanded Nancy, bluntly.

"Hush! Sh-hh! Whish-th!" hissed Rosa, her sibilant sounds imitating the desired silence. "Don't you know, pretty Coz, that's the Great Secret?"

"What Great Secret?" Nancy flung up her head defiantly.

"Mine," replied Rosa crisply. "Here's the trays."

For some moments Nancy showed her feelings, in fact, she almost pouted, for, she decided, if Rosa was going to keep up this attitude of mystery, and keep hinting at things, what fun was she, Nancy, going to have out of this long and almost lonely summer?

Possibly sensing her resentment, Rosa hurried to explain.

"When the folks are gone and we have

everything to ourselves," she began, "of course, things will be different."

Nancy brightened at this. Her cousin was a very different girl from all Nancy's other friends, it was only fair to give her a chance—a different sort of chance to what any other of Nancy's chums might have expected.

The dinner served on Rosa's pretty heart-shaped table proved a treat indeed.

"Lots more fun than eating in the dining room with Baldy at one's elbow," declared Nancy. "But it may seem strange to Betty—"

"Betty! She hasn't gone down either," replied Rosa. "Catch her sitting up straight for half an hour with only dear dad to applaud."

"Oh," echoed Nancy. "I'm glad she won't miss us, because mother warned me most particularly to be punctual at meals."

"Don't worry, love. They'll be gone early in the morning, then we can eat our meals on the rocks—if you're not afraid of lizards, snakes, chipmunks and otters."

"I'm not," said Nancy, dryly.

"You promised to tell me about last summer," Rosa reminded her. "How you got won over to the cooking class scheme."

"Oh, yes," and Nancy started in on her orange sherbert just as she started in on the story. "Well, you see, we have always kept rather busy. We live that way. It wouldn't be fair to let mother work in the library while Ted and I just—ran loose—"

"Why wouldn't it?" asked Rosa innocently. "You two kids couldn't work in a library."

"No, but we could learn how to do something," fended Nancy. "Mother didn't learn just how to do that either, she simply did it because she knew she should."

"Oh, yes, certainly," spoke up Rosa rather apologetically. "Don't think that I don't appreciate your mother, Nance. Dad thinks she's the best little woman there is, but I just didn't understand."

"There are a lot of things that neither of us understand," answered Nancy, suddenly digressing. "I suppose it is because you and I have such different lives. There I live in a Massachusetts town and have only spent my summers at little places just outside, while you—"

"I don't live anywhere," moaned Rosa. "I just go from one place to the other like a suit-case or a hat box. School in Connecticut, winters in New York or maybe Boston, vacations in the craziest places in the world, until this summer. I just insisted upon staying here in my own dear mother's place. She *loved* Fernlode."

Gulping on the confection which she should not have eaten, Rosa showed genuine love for the mother who had gone. Respecting her feelings, it was some time before Nancy broke the silence, but when she did so it was of that jolly summer—last summer—at Long Leigh that she talked. She told Rosa all about the Whatnot Shop, about dear little Miss Manners, who had since become one of Nancy's family by making her simple, humble home with them, and gladly assuming such cares as Nancy's mother allowed her to take over.

The fun every one had in the cistern mystery just sent Rosa off into gales of laughter as Nancy told of it, and while this was the story of Nancy Brandon: Enthusiast, as told in volume one of this series, it was easy to understand how the two cousins enjoyed its telling.

Presently there was a tap at the door, then Margot entered.

"The Durand's are here—but you mustn't think of going out, Rosa—"

"I'm going!" threatened the girl with the bandaged ankle, again up "in arms."

CHAPTER IX

THE CURE FOR QUARRELS

As if to make positive that she intended to do exactly as she pleased, especially if the doing of it were opposed by the anxious Margot, Rosa rushed to dress.

"I've been in long enough," she assured Nancy, "I'd die if I were cooped up here any longer. I phoned Gar, told him the doctor said I had to go out—"

"Rosa!" Nancy's manner showed more disappointment than shock.

"Now, Nannily, don't go getting excited. My ankle wasn't bad, really. It was just fun to have a lot of attention. You have no idea how precious little of it I get, usually."

Nancy sighed. Her own vivid personality felt eclipsed beside the turbulent, changeable cousin. She, Nancy, simply had to be polite and accept things as Rosa offered them, but with each new turn she found herself more and more baffled. Even if she were company and had to appear pleased with things, she was feeling rather tired of Rosa's whims. They weren't funny at all; not half so funny as just anything that Ted would do. But why think of Ted now? He was having a fine time with boys at a boys' camp, and Nancy was wishing she had gone to a girls' camp with Ruth Ashley.

"What are you going to put on?" asked Rosa very casually, too casually to be taken as Rosa tried to make it.

"I'm not going to change," replied Nancy. "I'm not going out."

"Not going out!" exclaimed Rosa, as if such a contingency had never occurred to her. "Why, Nancy *I'm* going."

"Go ahead," said Nancy. This was casual.

"But *I* want you to come," Rosa's voice was a key higher.

"Sorry, but *I* don't want to go."

Following that surprising statement Rosa rushed around, tossing helpless garments from one end of the room to another, as if taking her spite out on them. She wasn't saying a word to Nancy; Nancy wasn't saying a word to her.

Presently Margot came in for the trays, and as she gathered things up she made known her disapproval of Rosa's conduct.

"I don't like to scold, Rosalind, when your cousin has just come, and your father is leaving—"

"Oh, go ahead and scold, Maggie," said Rosa impertinently. "Get it out of your system. Your eyes look bulgy and—"

"Rosalind! I will not take any impudence. You know that," replied Margot quite properly. "You may be too big to be put in a corner, but you *would* miss your allowance, and I've got to have some control of you if I am to be responsible for your welfare."

At this threat, that her allowance would be withheld if she did not do better, Rosa quieted down—some. She stopped throwing things around but she did not speak to Nancy. Neither did Nancy speak to her. In fact, she felt like doing almost anything else, for her vacation was being spoiled just because Rosa was so obstinate.

If only she hadn't come! If only she had gone with patient little Miss Manners, who loved her. Certainly Rosa couldn't care anything about her and treat her this way.

Once Nancy started on this line of reasoning the inevitable was bound to happen. In feeling sorry for herself she was going to become homesick!

"I should think you would be ashamed—" began Margot, but Rosa checked her.

"I am, if that's any good to know. I'm always ashamed, but *you* don't have to make it worse, Margot."

Nancy glanced over at Rosa, who was doing what she usually did in dressing: trying to make her waist line look smaller by actually making it look larger. She was pulling a girdle in so tight that the rebellious little bunches of flesh pouched out in pudgy pockets above and below.

She was ashamed—of being too fat! As Nancy realized this her resentment cooled.

She did love Rosalind and perhaps Rosalind loved her. Just because Rosa was too stout and not wise enough to understand that such a thing has little, if anything, to do with personality, her young life was being embittered. She imagined that every one slighted her; that every one laughed at her; that every one was making fun of her. Whereas, she was only a growing girl with her growth unbalanced.

The dark blue dress that Rosa was adjusting might have been a school uniform in the severity of its lines; but Rosa had declared she could only wear dark colors; that Orilla had told her so.

The longer both girls held silence against each other, the harder it was going to be to break it. Nancy was not ungenerous, but she was human, and no girl wants to "give in" when she feels herself to have been the one injured. Margot noticed this set expression, and the girls' lack of conversation. Also, she noticed Nancy biting her lip.

"Not quarreling with your cousin, I hope, Rosalind," said the woman severely. "I do believe I shall have to have a talk with your father."

"He'd love it," scoffed Rosa, saucily.

"Very well," said Margot with finality, "I shall."

The butler had been in twice for the trays and now everything was cleared away. Rosa was dressed, hatted and coated, and she was only pretending to fuss with her hair. Nancy jumped up and with a hasty "I'm going to read, Rosa," flew into her own room.

She knew this would make matters worse; that the only time to stop a quarrel is before it starts, but Nancy was not equal, just then, to reasonable arguments. All she could see, feel or know, was that she wished she were almost any place else than at Fernlode.

Being away from home, visiting and having things unpleasant! It was so easy to bring tears to her eyes now, and she so rarely cried at home. She just had to choke back the tears that were forcing themselves up her throat and trying to reach her eyes.

Why should she have been made so miserable? Why was Rosa so unreasonable? What if she was fat, wasn't Nancy thin? Didn't her friends always call her "skinny" and she hadn't even bothered about it any more than she had fussed over the "Nincy-niney-nanny-notey in a red petticoaty," Ted's fighting chant or battle cry, as their mother always termed his childish taunt.

Rosa was going downstairs—Nancy heard her grumbling as she went, and it seemed Margot had carried out her threat, for Rosa was talking back and scoffing at the commands evidently sent by her father.

"Serves her right!" was Nancy's first impulsive criticism. Then again came the thought of Ted. How she and he would quarrel, how she would declare she hoped her mother would do all sorts of things to him (which, of course, she never did), and then in the end, just as Ted was realizing that something in the way of discipline might possibly be visited upon him, Nancy would always relent. She would even step between him and the impending evil.

That was exactly how she felt now. After all, Rosa was such a baby. She hadn't learned from contact with companions, for, according to her own story, she had never had a real chum.

"Ted, Ted, Ted!" kept persistingly challenging Nancy, until she knew she would have to do something for Rosa. It was not being generous, really, it was just doing what she had been brought up to do—to be brave enough to be humble.

She flew to her mirror and daubbed at her eyes; they looked rather puckery. Then she flirted her powder puff around her nose, that looked decidedly shiny.

"Wish I had put on my red dress," she told her reflection in the glass, "but there's no time now. If I run along with Rosa, surely Uncle Frederic won't scold her."

On the broad stair landing, where the big brass lanterns and the lovely soft palms opened the way into the living room, she found the surprised Rosa.

"Why, Nancy!" she exclaimed. "I thought—"

"But I don't care for that book," said Nancy evasively. "Where are you going?"

"Horrid old Margot—"

"Hush! Let's make believe we're—where's Dell? I thought she was here."

"Gone. She was here. Dad said I couldn't go out. They're going to the park—" Rosa's voice was full of rancor.

"Can't we go out in the cove in your flat-bottom boat? I love to row, and it's safe in the cove, isn't it?" asked Nancy, glad to think of a reasonable plan.

"Too safe. Like swimming doll ducks in the bath tub. But we'll go. I'll ask dad. He—has—summoned me—"

Just then, down the long hall strode the gentleman in question. He was waving a paper at Nancy.

"A letter for you, Antoinette," he announced gaily. "A steamer letter from your mother—"

"Oh, goody!" exclaimed Nancy happily. "Come on, Rosa. Let's read it."

"But dad wants to see me—"

"Oh, never mind, Boots," he replied, just giving the willful one a playful shake. "Give dad a kiss and promise—promise to be good."

Whereat Rosa actually sprang upon the foot with the injured ankle, hugging her father so impulsively that Nancy instantly decided she was just like Ted.

Is there anything lovelier than the calm after the storm? Arm in arm Rosa and Nancy sauntered off, their happy laughter ringing through old Fernlode, their voices blending in genuine affection until reaching the water's edge, Rosa showed Nancy how she "megaphoned" down the lake to No Man's Land, a little island, desolate and alone. Nancy did the phoning by cupping her hands and shouting in the weird way that always provokes an echo.

"Ted was such a funny little fellow when he was very small," Nancy told her cousin. "He used to say he loved to go under bridges, where he could hear his voice after he was finished with it."

"Finished with it?" queried Rosa.

"Yes; that's the way he used to describe an echo."

"Oh, how funny!" yelled Rosa. "Let's give a couple of echoes for Ted."

They shouted again and again, until the echoes became a mere jumble of sounds.

"I must read Mumsey's letter," insisted Nancy presently. "Just let's sit in the boat and—read it."

The steamer letter proved the treat it was bound to be, Nancy hugging every word, every syllable, while Rosa leaned over, fascinated.

"Your mother is—wonderful, Nan," she said finally. "No wonder you—you've got so much sense."

"Have I?" asked Nancy, unwilling to take that sort of compliment. "No one, not any of my friends, ever say things like that to me; I'm so flighty," she admitted quite frankly.

"But you're not scrappy like I am," spoke Rosa. "I just wonder why I love to—oppose folks." This little sentence sounded tragic from Rosa's lips. Her round, dimpily face fell into serious lines as she expressed this query, and even her baby-blue eyes looked far away where they could see nothing.

"You're not scrappy," Nancy felt bound to defend. "Maybe you just imagine folks are opposing you," she hazarded.

"I know they are," insisted Rosa sadly.

CHAPTER X

MAROONED AT NIGHTFALL

It was Nancy who now felt guilty—guilty of arousing in Rosa that queer little spirit of rebellion which seemed to rule her budding life.

"But, Rosa," she argued, quite helplessly, for Nancy had no illusion about her own weaknesses, "don't you think, maybe, you just imagine a lot of things?"

"Don't you?" fired back Rosa.

"No, not that way," replied Nancy. "What's the use of making worries? If you had a brother like our Ted—"

"Or a sister like Ted has," put in Rosa good-humoredly. "I know you hate silly stuff, Nancy. You wouldn't let me say that you've done me a lot of good already; but you have."

"How? Why, Rosa, we hardly know each other, and I really couldn't do you good, for

I'm rather—rather queer, you know. I just couldn't—" Nancy stumbled and paused.

"Pretend," finished Rosa. "That's it, Nancy, you're just being queer, is the reason. There's a name for it but don't let's bother about that. Shall we row out?"

"I love to row," declared Nancy again, taking her place at the oars.

"And I hate to," admitted Rosa, settling back in the cushions.

"Rowing ought to be good for you," suggested Nancy. "Isn't it queer how we skinnies always do the things that make us thinner?"

"And we fatties—" But Rosa's remark was cut short by a call; it seemed to come from the island.

"What's that!" both girls exclaimed.

They listened.

"It's coming from No Man's Land and it's a woman's voice," declared Rosa.

"Can we row over there?" asked Nancy. "She's in distress, surely."

"Maybe *you* could, but I can't row worth a

cent," confessed Rosa. "I'll answer her."

She again cupped her hands to her mouth and called the megaphone call.

"Whoo-hoo! Where are—you!"

"Here! Here!" came a shrill reply. "On the island! Come—get—me!"

"Guess we'll have to try," sighed Rosa. "I suppose it's some one marooned out there and naturally afraid of night coming. It might storm to-night, too."

Without further ado Nancy turned the boat and headed for the island. The dot of land was not more than a dark speck on the sunset-lighted waters, for although it was late evening, the glow of a parting day was still gloriously strewn over the great, broad lake and mountains, flanking every side of the basin and adding to its depths. The usual craft were rather scarce just now, social dinner-times absorbing the lure of the great Out Doors.

Valiantly Nancy tugged at her oars, while Rosa directed verbally and steered at the helm. The distance was much longer than it had appeared to be, but after safely passing Dead Rock and Eagles' Lair, the little boat was now bravely skirting the island.

"Here! Here!" called a woman's voice shrilly. "Thank the mercies you've come! I thought I was here for the night and I've got to—"

"Oh, hello, Mrs. Pixley!" exclaimed Rosa. "So it's you! However did you get caught over here?"

"I didn't—didn't get caught at all. It was that brazen girl—"

"Orilla?" asked Rosa.

"No one else. Just Orilla. The sassy little thing—"

Nancy was just pulling in to land when it seemed to her that the voice sounded oddly familiar. Then she caught sight of the excited woman's face.

"Oh, hello!" she too exclaimed. "You're the lady with the grape juice bottle—the one that exploded in the train!" Nancy declared in astonishment.

"Of all things! I want to know! And

you're the little girl who tried to help me! Rosalind Fernell, is this girl visiting you?" demanded she whom Rosa had called Mrs. Pixley.

"Why, of course. She's my cousin, Nancy Brandon from out Boston way. How did *you* know her?"

A rather sketchy account of the train incident was then furnished in a dialogue between Nancy and Mrs. Pixley, the latter at the same time gathering up pails and baskets and preparing to get into the boat.

"I came over here for berries," she explained. "I've a sick lady who would have blueberries, and I knew I'd get them here. Orilla had the launch—Mr. Cowan's, you know, Rosa, and she ran me over here like a streak. Promised to be back by five but here it is—What time is it, anyway?"

"Nearly nine," replied Rosa. "What do you suppose happened to Orilla?"

"Nothing. Nothing *could* happen to her. I often tell her mother I don't see what's going to become of that girl. Shall I get in the front? I don't want to spill them blueberries. There's hardly any ripe yet, but Miss Sandford has been pestering me for some. There, now I'm all right. Want me to row? It's such a mercy you came. No boats came past the island—hardly any, and I'm hoarse from shoutin'. Here, young lady, give me them oars. You're tuckered out," and still talking Mrs. Pixley took Nancy's place, not against Nancy's will, either.

"But Orilla," Rosa said again. "I haven't seen Cowan's launch out this afternoon. And she always comes by our dock when she has that out."

"Don't you bother with that girl, Rosalind," cautioned Mrs. Pixley. "She's flighty. Never no telling what she's going to do next—"

"But she's awfully smart," interrupted Rosa.

"In some ways, but that don't make her wise." Mrs. Pixley was an expert at the oars as well as being a fluent talker. Nancy watched and listened, with admiration and with interest.

"I'll go in at your place, Rosalind," continued the woman, "and get a ride down the road. Lots of cars running down the hill at this time of night. And if you see Orilla Rigney you can tell her for me, she'll not get another drop of milk at my place. To play me such a trick!" Mrs. Pixley's indignation almost interfered with her talking, but not quite.

"Just imagine you knowing Mrs. Pixley, Nancy," Rosalind managed to remark as they pulled in.

"Yes, just imagine!" repeated the woman before Nancy could speak. "Well, if you ever saw that grape juice fly, Rosalind, you'd understand how well *I* got acquainted on that car!"

"How funny!" persisted Rosa. "Did it hurt anyone?"

"Not exactly anyone, but a lot of things," laughed the woman. "I'll never forget that fat man's shirt front! Looked like my log-cabin quilt. And the lady with the yellow hair—remember her, Nancy? How it turned lavender?"

"Indeed I do; she looked like someone made up for a masquerade—"

"I wish I'd been there!" sighed Rose, interrupting Nancy. "But I never happen to be around when that sort of lark is on. Well, here we are. All ashore who's going ashore!" she chanted. "And Mrs. Pixley, you can row almost as well as Nancy."

This compliment was accepted with another flood of words from Mrs. Pixley. When all were again safely landed at the Fernell dock, the queer woman took herself off without any unnecessary delay. She had talked of her experiences on the train when Nancy had witnessed the grape juice explosion, she had talked of and against Orilla Rigney, she had talked of the unreasonable "lady customer" who had insisted upon early blueberries, and Nancy wondered, as she listened to her repeat her thanks and her goodnights, if Mrs. Pixley really ever stopped talking.

But this was not the most interesting point in the little adventure. Nancy's wonderment centered more about the connection of

Orilla with the affair. Mrs. Pixley seemed one more person who disliked that girl, and Nancy said so to Rosa.

"Wasn't it dreadful of Orilla not to go back for her?" she said, when she and Rosa tied up the boat.

"It wouldn't have killed old Pixley to stay on the island all night," defended Rosa. "Maybe it would have cooled off her gabbing."

Nancy had no desire to start a fresh argument. So she did not press the subject further, but she wondered when this person of mystery would make her appearance in Rosa's home. That the passage for Europe of Mr. and Mrs. Fernell, now only a few hours off, would precipitate the invasion of Orilla, seemed rather too sure a guess for Nancy, for she dreaded its realization. She didn't want anything to do with the Rigney girl, and she hoped Rosa would not now find her companionship desirable.

For in Nancy's mind was stored the vivid remembrance of Rosa's accident in the woods.

This she could not help attributing to Orilla's queer influence, and she hoped that the painful affair had been a good lesson to Rosa.

"Afraid of the dark?" Rosa asked, as the last rays of light were caught up in the receding sky.

"No, not of the dark," replied Nancy, trying again the knot with which she fastened the boat. "But it certainly is lonely out here, with all that water to run into if anyone chases us," she added, jokingly.

"You bet!" agreed Rosa. "That's one thing we must never try to do; we must not try to run across that lake, for it's awfully wet."

"Is that a boat I hear? Maybe it's Orilla," suggested Nancy, listening to the distant purr of a motor boat.

"No, I don't believe it is," replied Rosa. "You see, she keeps awfully busy, and I suppose it didn't worry her any to leave poor Pixley to swim ashore."

"What a very odd girl she must be," continued Nancy, almost against her will.

"Perhaps she is, but then—oh, well, don't let's bother about her. Dad is sure to be watching the moon rise from the East porch," said Rosa, as they started back toward the house. "Let's go talk to him."

"But perhaps he and—"

"Oh, Betty will be bossing the packing," interrupted Rosa, anticipating the words of Nancy's objections. "Come on. I'm going to miss dad and I want to be with him all I can—now."

"Then *you* go talk to him, Rosa," urged Nancy, considerately. "I've got some things to do. You won't mind. You see, I must write mother at once, so that she'll get it almost as soon as she reaches London."

"Give her my love," said Rosa, as the cousins parted on the porch.

On the little table in her room Nancy found a gift from Betty, a beautiful rainbow chiffon scarf, and also a big box of candy from her Uncle Frederic. She loved the scarf; it was beautiful, and would blend with any and every costume. The candy, of course, was equally welcome, for she had no doubt that her uncle himself had thought of it.

Standing before the broad mirror of her dresser she tried on the scarf. Her simple powder-blue dress was made much more attractive beneath its colorful folds, and it delighted Nancy to vision its possibilities as an adjunct to her limited outfit. It would be lovely over her apple green—the black shadows in it would be wonderful over green, she reflected, and her gray dress—the one she wanted so much and her mother objected to because of its somberness—that would be perfect with the rainbow scarf.

Throwing the filmy ends first over one shoulder and then over the other, stepping this way and that to suit the pose and get just the correct lighting on the scarf, Nancy was quite unconscious of a light step approaching her open door.

Then, as she turned once more to try just one more swing of the silken tie, she found herself facing the smiling Lady Betty.

CHAPTER XI

TRYING ON IDEALISM

Fully expecting Mrs. Frederic Fernell to pour into her ears the story of Rosa's rebellious habits, with the intention of soliciting Nancy's aid toward their correction, Nancy instantly assumed the defensive. She did not come out to New Hampshire to reform Rosalind Fernell, and besides that, she was not ready to admit that Rosa needed reforming.

All of which really marked Nancy's sincerity, for she was by no means a "poser." She knew she had failings herself, so why should not Rosa have some? Because each differed in her weakness, did that make either less weak or less troublesome? Not according to Nancy's reasoning, at any rate.

The figure floating into her room, as usual sent a dainty fragrance on ahead.

"I'm so glad you like your scarf, dear," said

Betty, sinking into the nearest chair, "and I see you do."

"Oh, I love it," said Nancy, forgetting everything else but her gratitude. "Thank you so much for giving it to me—Betty." She always paused before using the name without any other distinguishing mark of respect.

"I knew it would match you—you are so varied in your own tones. Well, my dear, I do so want you to have a lovely time with Rosa this summer, that I just stepped in to assure you of that. Your Uncle Frederic and I are most anxious to have both of you enjoy yourselves. To help you to do so, we have made some new plans." The chair with the parrot cushion suited Betty best, so she sank into that as gracefully as usual.

Nancy caressed the playful scarf she still held about her shoulders and she, also, sat down. New plans! She hoped they would not be so very different, for she was only now becoming acquainted at Fernlode, and rather dreaded the unusual.

"It can be terribly dull here," pursued the

lady, "and for two young girls especially. So I have coaxed my husband to allow Rosa and you to attend little affairs at our hotel—properly chaperoned, of course," she concluded.

"At the Sunset Hotel?" queried Nancy, a little uneasily. She had no clothes suitable for such functions, was what she instantly thought.

"Yes, my dear. You see, your Uncle Frederic has implicit faith in the good judgment of our friends the Durands, and they will go with you—they always do attend the Sunset," said Lady Betty.

"That's lovely, of course," faltered Nancy, "but mother had no idea—"

"I understand, dear child," interrupted the little queen in her lace robes in the big chair. "You shall need pretty things, and I just *love* to buy them, so I've had a box sent in to you. You see, Rosa," as Nancy was attempting to speak, "has an idea no one can buy anything for *her*. She is stout, but young enough to grow thin," said the remote step-mother, "yet, I can't interfere with Rosa. It just makes her more furious."

"It's lovely of you to bother with me, Betty, and I do like pretty things. But I hate to give you so much bother." Nancy felt very stupid making such commonplace thanks. Ted would have choked to listen to that foolish speech. Was Betty going to avoid the troublesome subject of Rosa's tempers? Was Nancy going to escape the tactful lecture she had felt sure of receiving?

"If things have to be altered Margot will attend to that," went on the Lady Betty, "and you just *wear* everything. That's what they're for. Have a good time and grow fat! Wouldn't it be wonderful if some little fairy took from Rosa what she gave to you?"

"I suppose we both could afford at least some of that sort of change," said Nancy, warming up to Betty's pleasantries. "But if I had just known what clothes I should have needed, I am sure I would have brought them along."

"Then, I'm glad you didn't know. Otherwise I should have missed all the fun of my shopping tour. Folks think me very vain, I know," admitted the pretty Mrs. Fernell, "but I do *love* beautiful things. I'd like to dress a whole army of girls—"

"But not like soldiers," ventured Nancy.

"Like the prettiest soldiers in all ages—the girls who fight the battles of wanting things they deserve, yet cannot always have." In this rather confused speech, even Nancy could see that Betty was trying to avoid reference to her own (Nancy's) possible needs.

"You are very kind, indeed," said Nancy quietly.

"Not really. Because, you see, my dear, I have given myself so much pleasure. But I hope things will fit and that you will like—most of them."

"I'm sure to," declared Nancy. Then as Betty stood up she asked:

"Isn't anything in the box for Rosa? If I see that she likes anything may I say you would like her to have it?"

"You clever child!" laughed the lady, and Nancy's admiration for her charms increased with the flow of silvery sounds. "You are really an idealist; you must have everything ideally arranged," she finished.

"But I am not, really," protested Nancy, now actually sensing the dreaded lecture.

Nancy felt rather foolish, as any girl would, in spite of the way Betty complimented her, for back of it all she was sure, quite positive the real point of the talk lay in the need of Rosa for healthy companionship. Not that Nancy wasn't grateful for the confidence and for the gifts, but because she really wasn't "an old lady" and hated anything that made her feel like one.

"Rosa is with her daddy now, so I'm stealing this little chat with you," was Mrs. Fernell's next remark. "I do love Rosa—all our family always loved her mother," said Betty, much to Nancy's surprise. "My sister was Katherine's school chum, and that's how Fred and I became acquainted."

"Oh," replied Nancy, the single syllable embodying her surprise.

"Yes." A deep sigh from Betty was also

significant. "But Rosa has proved a problem. She resents, it seems, my marrying her father, although I have tried quietly to show her how little I intend to interfere with her life."

She knew it would come; it just had to, and she couldn't have expected to escape it, although at the moment Nancy hated her position as confidante, against her most loyal feelings for Rosa. That was just it; she couldn't escape it. Presently her care of Rosa would be thrust at her, just as if she had been some kind of nurse.

"It will work out all right; I'm sure, however," went on the pretty one, "if only we can keep Rosa away from certain influences. You see, Nancy, this is an unpleasant topic for me, naturally," and the soft voice fell into deep blue velvet tones, "but as I am going away, and as I really do stand very close to Rosalind, I feel you should understand."

"Yes," was all Nancy could think of saying.

"There was a girl here—you have probably heard of her, Orilla Rigney," began Mrs. Fernell again, although she was still standing, "and she is responsible for much of Rosa's aggressiveness. You see, she and her mother lived here as sort of care-takers, and your Uncle Frederic was so kind to them they felt the place was and should be their home. The girl has tried to injure me ever since I came here. As if I could have anything in common with them." Here Mrs. Fernell paused, haughtily. "Unfortunately she has gotten into Rosa's confidence, with a lot of silly nonsense," she continued after a moment. "Well, Nancy, you see I am piling troubles upon your head, but Rosa is a great baby in spite of her decided ways. So just have a good time, wear the pretty clothes, and when you write to your mother tell her we hope to find her in the big country across the water. Frederic Fernell thinks his sister is just one woman without equal, and I feel I know her through his admiration and love—"

This sudden turn in the glimpse of Betty's character left Nancy simply gasping with surprise. She wasn't at all the foolish, pretty doll she had been pictured, she *did* love Rosa, and Rosa was simply crazy to be so opposed to her, thought Nancy.

One thing was certain, however, nobody, just nobody, had a good word for Orilla. Jealousy is an awful thing, Nancy reflected, for even in her short life she had heard of its offences and, of course, Orilla was jealous.

Before Rosa returned from her confab with her father and before Lady Betty was back in her own room, Nancy had again fallen into speculation as to when, where and how she would actually meet Orilla.

"When the coast is clear," she promptly decided. "When the folks are gone and Rosa is alone. But *I'll* be here," decided Nancy, not realizing how promptly she was espousing the cause she had been so determined to ignore.

Then a thumping and pouncing through the hall announced the arrival of Rosa. She was calling to Nancy, shouting, yelling without even expecting or even giving Nancy the slightest chance of replying.

"What do you know! What do you know!" she sang out joyously. "We're going to the hotel! Down to Sunset! Nancy Brandon, what a lark! In the dark! Let us park!" she went on foolishly, trying to rhyme words to suit her caprice. "If you hadn't come, of course," she brought her voice down a few keys but not quite to dead center, "I shouldn't have been allowed that. Betty has fallen in love with you—"

"Don't be silly, Rosa," said Nancy quite sagely. "It's all on your account and you're a perfect goose not to know that she is in love with *you*!"

"With me! Fat, furious me! With the bad tempered manners, and badness cropping out all over me!" scoffed Rosa.

"Like the bad boy in the play who was always scared to death of a pop gun. Rosa, you are not a very good actress," laughed Nancy, and in that little speech she showed Rosa the way that she, at least, regarded her faults. They were a pose, a manner put on to ward off sympathy. And Rosa herself could not hate sympathy more than did Nancy.

They talked over the prospects of that summer hotel until it would seem all the summer's fun and good times were dependent upon it. Rosa just couldn't wait to see what Betty was sending in from Boston in the box, which Nancy had tactfully said was "for us," and it was then, just as Betty had hinted, that Rosa forgot her rebel pose, for she actually expressed great hopes of what might be in that box for *her*!

"I have to do everything so quietly, so as not to arouse her suspicion," Betty had said. And now Nancy was hoping that she too would be able to follow that policy.

Nancy Brandon might indeed be an idealist, but she was blissfully ignorant of possessing any such subtle quality.

CHAPTER XII

WOODLAND RAMBLES

The next day went by in a whirl. After seeing the folks off for Europe—Nancy and Rosa went over to Mount Major, where Mr. and Mrs. Fernell took the New York train—the remaining hours seemed too few in which to crowd all the things Rosa had planned to do.

The injured foot was all but forgotten. Never was a girl livelier than Rosa, more enthusiastic nor more expectant—for the great times ahead. But through all her plans, it seemed to Nancy, a vein of mystery ran. For instance, she would talk about losing weight, exercising, dieting and go over the entire formula, when suddenly she would stop short, maybe put her finger to her lips and do something to indicate secrecy.

"It's all planned and plotted," she declared, when she finally did agree to take a little walk through the special fern path from which the place had received its name, "and won't daddy and Betty be surprised?"

"What makes you so sure?" asked Nancy. "How ever can you tell that you will lose pounds and pounds?"

"I'm *positive,*" replied Rosa. "And I just dream of it all the time. Haven't you ever had that sort of dream?"

"The silly kind? Surely. I had one special pet—and I'm afraid I haven't banished it yet," admitted Nancy. "I always wanted to wake up with light golden curls and heavenly blue eyes."

The shout with which Rosa replied to this must have disturbed every pixy in the woods, for she simply roared!

"And you think *that* would make you happy! Why, I have blue eyes and curls, and my hair was golden—"

"And you are very pretty!"

"Nancy—Antoinette Brandon!"

"I mean it. You are!"

"Fat me!"

"You don't have to stay fat!"

"I'm *not* going to!"

"Rosa—Rosalind Fernell!"

"What?"

"Please tell me what you mean."

"By getting thin?"

"No. How are you going to get thin?"

"Oh." Rosa swung herself around until she touched the little white birch tree with her finger tips. "You just wait and see!"

"I think that's rather mean." Nancy also swung herself around but not in Rosa's direction. "I do hope you are not going to do anything foolish."

"That depends. *Margot* thinks everything I do is foolish."

"Oh, you know I don't mean that, Rosa," Nancy answered quickly. "But, you see, with the folks away we've got to be rather—cautious."

"Now, don't preach."

"I don't know how. Ted says I preach like the umpire at a ball game."

"You were going to show me his funny letter," put in Rosa, her eagerness to change the subject not even thinly disguised. "I know you have a whole batch of them, too. You know, Dell is just crazy about that sort of thing. She wants to teach kindergarten. Just imagine!"

"She's very intelligent," said Nancy, falling back into her own way of saying things which had ever been a part of her home life. "Mother always says we can tell folks by the things they prefer, rather than by the company they keep."

"You're over my head, Nancy," laughed Rosa. "But if that's true I must be a spiritual skeleton, for I love—thin folks." Impulsively Rosa had thrown her arms around Nancy, and just as impulsively Nancy had thrown her arms around Rosa, until presently they were dancing through the woods like a couple of sprites—even if Rosa was a trifle out of spritely proportion.

They sang snatches of songs, they tried out different steps and were as free as the air about them; until they heard something queer.

"What's that?" Nancy asked the question first.

"I wonder," replied Rosa.

"Sounds like someone groaning."

"A man, don't you think?" Rosa's voice had dwindled to a whisper.

Again came the noise interrupting their questions. This time there was no mistaking it. Someone was groaning.

"Let's run back; we're away out in Baker's Woods," said Rosa with deep concern. "And there's the road. We'll take that," at which both girls turned to the well beaten path.

"Halt!" came the command. "Right about face!"

"Garry Durand!" exclaimed Rosa. "You mean thing!"

"Not to be an old tramp or something?" jeered the boy, who had stepped out into their path and was enjoying the little fright he had given them. "I suppose," he went on, "you are disappointed. A real bandit would have been more fun."

"Now, Gar," scolded Rosa, "you know a

lot better than that. We were just wondering where you and Dell had been keeping yourselves."

"Like fun you were, just wondering. We've been watching you dance. What was that? A new one?"

"We?" queried Rosa.

"Yes. Come on, Paul; get introduced."

At this there stepped from behind a big tree, another young man—no doubt Paul.

"This is Paul Randolph," said Gar, "Miss Brandon and the famous Rosa—"

But Rosa cut that short. "The idea," she protested, "of you peeping."

"We weren't, really," defended Paul. "We just came along. Our car went dry and we were walking back."

"Then, we'll forgive you," Nancy managed to say. She was losing the natural self-consciousness which had at first been difficult to overcome. Coming from the home of her devoted mother and darling Ted into the confused surroundings of Rosa, this was easy to understand.

As she spoke Paul stepped up to her, and they started off in the direction of home. Rosa was ahead with Gar and she, it appeared, was not in agreement with him. He argued and she protested.

Instantly his remark about Nancy coming just in time to save Rosa from some mysterious danger, flitted back into Nancy's mind. It had been said at their very first meeting, but as time wore on, many other things appeared to make it seem important, and, of course, it was connected with Orilla. Now, Nancy could scarcely keep track of what Paul was saying, because of the distraction ahead with Rosa and Gar.

"I tell you flatly I won't!" Gar broke out once just as Rosa, smiling, grabbed his arm and turned the remark into a joke. But as he turned around facing Nancy and Paul, his expression flatly belied Rosa's attempt.

"Did you hear about the fun we are going to have at Sunset?" Rosa asked Paul.

"Hear about the *fun* you are *going* to have?" he teased. "How could we?"

"Oh, you know what I mean," pouted Rosa. "We are going to the dances."

"So are we," said Paul gallantly, "so I suppose that's hearing about the fun we are *all* going to have."

"They have swell music," put in Gar. "The best banjoist in Boston is with that outfit."

"But really it isn't Sunset that's so attractive, but getting out," explained Rosa. "You see, I've been rather tied to the apron string of Margot—"

"Lovely long string," said Paul gaily, "judging from Gar's accounts."

"Has he been giving away my secrets?" asked Rosa, winking at Nancy and attempting to strike Gar.

"Better be careful," cautioned Nancy, "or you'll give them away yourself, Rosa. That's the worst of having secrets; they're so tricky."

"Now we're getting interesting," remarked Paul. "Go ahead, Nancy. Give us your idea of—secrets."

"Oh, she hasn't any," put in Rosa, rather flustered. "That is, she hasn't any of my kind; she doesn't have to."

Everybody laughed at that except Rosa, and even to Paul Randolph, the stranger, Rosa's uneasiness must have been evident. Quickly deciding to save her cousin from further embarrassment, Nancy broke into a lively talk about New Hampshire, comparing it with Massachusetts, and insisting that the big, measureless lake, with mountains all around it, and according to tradition with mountains hidden in its depth, was no more scenically beautiful than many another less famous and much smaller lake in the sister state.

"I'll show you scenery," declared Gar in worthy defense of his adopted territory. "Over among those hills there's everything you could imagine in the way of rocks and lands and vegetation—"

"Except pretty wild flowers," cut in Nancy. "And you don't even have very pretty ferns."

Whereat a general study in the ferns all around them was begun. The little by-play helped to make talk and the interest shown was surely genuine, although occasionally Rosa would step aside with Gar and insist upon whispering to him. Nancy tried to keep up her contention that New Hampshire ferns were not as lacy as those of Massachusetts, but the argument going on between Rosa and Gar was hard to close her ears to.

"Say!" called out Paul suddenly, kicking over a big bunch of "umbrella fungus," "what's going on between you two anyway? Don't you want an umpire?"

"No," fired back Gar, "a referee would be better. Rosa thinks because I'm an old friend she can get me into her sort of scrapes. You've no idea, Nancy," he sighed playfully, "how many scrapes Rosa *can* get into."

"Oh, you think you're smart, don't you?" snapped Rosa, childishly. "Just because—because I happen to have different plans from yours, Gar."

"But we're helpless, you know, Rosa," Nancy hurried to say. "We only got permission to go out without Margot, on condition that we would be very good and do everything that Dell and Gar wanted us to do."

"As if I intend to follow that silly stuff," flung back Rosa, defiantly.

"Oh, all right," drawled Gar elaborately, as if he were being very much offended. "Don't worry about us. We can find plenty to do without—"

"Peace! Peace!" chanted Paul, as if fearful that the fun might result otherwise. "We might want an umpire or even a referee, but we don't want a policeman."

"Well, how about it?" asked Gar, turning so suddenly to another trend of thought that Nancy didn't even guess what he meant. "Do we go to the dance to-night or don't we?"

"I can't go," declared Rosa, promptly.

"Oh, you know you can if you want to, Rose," the boy urged, "and it's going to be a big time."

"But we really don't take part in the dance, do we?" queried Nancy, just a little timidly, for she was not yet old enough to go to dances.

"Don't worry, lamb," said Rosa, facetiously, "even the very babes dance at summer hotels early in the evening. Later, of course, the grown-ups own the floor. What we want to see is the masquerade, the follies, and all the stunts they get up. They're fun!" she admitted, thus agreeing with Gar, who wanted to go to an affair that evening.

They were back to the porch of the big house now, and although Rosa pressed the boys to sit on the bench awhile, they politely declined, declaring they would presently have to go back to town for the delayed car.

Nancy was interested in Paul; it was so easy to talk to him—which fact Rosa presently explained.

"That's because he's so awfully smart," she said when Nancy remarked how much she liked him. "He's all ready for the M. I. T. I heard Gar say so."

"The Massachusetts Institute of Technology," amplified Nancy, "and he seems only like a high school boy."

"Just being smart does it," said Rosa cryptically. "One has either to be smart or handsome, and Paul is going to be both."

Margot came hurriedly out and interrupted them.

"I want to see you alone, Rosalind," she said, so severely that Nancy was glad to run off to her room and leave Rosa with her judge. She wondered what could be the matter that Margot would use such a tone, and look so indignantly at Rose.

"All right, Maggie," was all that Rosa said in reply to the peremptory summons.

CHAPTER XIII

A PARTY CAPE OF BLUE

It was two days later that the box of pretty things arrived from Boston. Nancy was glad that it had been addressed to Mrs. Frederic Fernell, for had her name been upon it, even under the other, she would not have known how to explain to Rosa.

And its coming brought a welcome relief in the feud which seemed to exist between Margot and Rosa, consequent upon that little private interview which had occurred after the walk in the woods.

Rosa had been sullen almost to the point of rudeness, but by this time Nancy had learned to regard her whims as mere childishness, a determination not "to give in" which was about as strong as good pie crust—and just as easily broken.

That Rosa's running off without giving an

account of her business was the real cause of Margot's misgivings, Nancy was now well aware, for Rosa would slip away without any explanation, about every time she found the chance of getting a ride into town without taking her own car, her own chauffeur, Margot or even Nancy.

At first this hurt Nancy's feelings. She was plainly being slighted. When Dell, Gar and Paul would come over or phone over for the girls to go off to see a tennis match, go swimming in the best part of the lake, which was some little distance from their cottages, or even go berrying, which was the thing Nancy best liked to do—to all or any of this Rosa would very likely find an excuse. And then, when some obscure person with a little flivver would happen along, she would suddenly remember something very important to be procured, and dash off.

Nancy was forming her own opinions of these unexplained flights. She noticed the messages that preceded them, she noticed Rosa trying to gather a certain amount of money, even asking Nancy to lend her a few dollars until she could cash her allowance, and she noticed more than any of these unfavorable symptoms, that Rosa had headaches, real severe headaches that made her cheeks burn, her eyes smart and feel altogether miserable—these always followed one of the flurried trips to town.

The advent of the box of pretty things was, therefore, a most welcome diversion, and now as Nancy and Rosa both tore off the wrappings, they chuckled merrily over what they hoped would be the contents.

"You must choose first," said Rosa generously. "You may have just whatever you like best."

Nancy was not sure that she would do this, and she felt almost guilty in her deception, for Mrs. Betty had very plainly said that the box was to be for Nancy.

Presently the papers had all been removed, the tissues torn apart, and there was then revealed such a gorgeous display of lovely, colorful things, that Rosa and Nancy fairly danced in delight over them.

"You take this," pressed Rosa. And then: "Oh, it must be for you, for it's too tiny for me." The article just referred to was a straight-line dress of tub silk, in a variegated stripe that was charming. Nancy took it, held it up and said how lovely she thought it was.

"And these undies," exclaimed Rosa again. "Betty must have bought those for you," as she passed over the dainty silk under things, "because I wear a special kind. These are lovely, though. Don't you think so?"

"Oh, they are be-u-tee-ful!" declared Nancy. "Hasn't Betty wonderful taste?"

"Yes, that's what she has the very most of—taste," said Rosa a little critically. "But then, she needs it. How would she look without it? Oh, see here!" as a little sport hat was dug out of its wrappings. "Now, someone has to have her hair bobbed," and she attempted to put the hat on her head. It stood up on top, as hats used to when women wore full skirts.

The girls went into gales of laughter at the effect. Then Nancy tried on the yellow felt hat, and, of course, it fitted her.

"For you again," declared Rosa, still happily expectant herself.

Then there was a darling little party dress of black roses in georgette, over yellow. This, obviously, was also for Nancy, until she began to feel embarrassed that nothing of Rosa's size was forthcoming.

Finally Rosa held up something blue. It was a cape—a lovely soft, fluffy cape of blue peach-blow cloth, trimmed with white fur.

"Oh! How darling!" both girls exclaimed in perfect harmony.

It was lovely. Almost like a piece of blue sky with a little fleecy cloud of white fur at the neck. Each of the girls held it; they fondled it, caressed it. Both of them loved it, it would fit both. Rosa decided she could wear *that*, and Nancy secretly tried to keep back the wish that she herself might have it.

She had always dreamed of just such a cape as that.

"It goes beautifully with my shade of hair, doesn't it," Rosa prattled. "And I adore that tone of blue. Oh, Nan, you can have everything else, but I'm so glad Betty thought to get this for me! I'm going to love her for it. Maybe I have been mean, as you say, Nan, and maybe Betty does love me, after all." And thereat the cape became the property of Rosa, while poor, disappointed Nancy applauded.

If ever a girl's heart can suddenly turn to ice and then try to choke her, that seemed to be what was happening just then to Nancy.

That cape! That precious, adorable cape, that she had always secretly dreamed of and that she could have made such wonderful use of! It was to her like a picture from her first fairy book.

Her mother or even Miss Manners (the loving "Manny" who was away off this summer) could have made dresses, pretty under things, and perhaps any of the other lovely articles, but a peach-blow cape, trimmed with white fur, seemed beyond the reach forever of poor Nancy.

"Don't you love it?" persisted Rosa, flirting around the glorious blue wings, like a great live bird.

"Yes, I do," said Nancy, too truthfully.

"I'm sorry now that we didn't plan to go down to the hotel to-night. I can't rest until I show this off. Not that I haven't a pretty party cape, for I have. Have you one, Nancy?"

"No, not yet," faltered Nancy. "I've never needed one."

"Then, you can have my red one. It will look stunning on you with your dark hair. It's called love-apple, that's tomato red, you know," explained Rosa, still flirting with the lovely new mantle.

"Oh, thank you, Rosa, but I really don't go to parties yet, you know," replied Nancy. She never cared for red in coats or capes, especially tomato red.

"It's quite gorgeous, with chiffon fliers, like wings when you walk. I'm sure none of your friends could have anything more elaborate—"

"That's just it, Rosa," interrupted Nancy,

"I couldn't wear things as elaborate as yours. They would look just as if you had given them to me."

"Oh, of course, if you feel that way about it; all right," replied the cousin a little stiffly. And that ended the discussion upon capes.

Somehow the joy that came in the box had exploded like a toy balloon, but Nancy tried to make herself think of the importance of Rosa's changed attitude toward Betty.

"If the cape does that," she prompted herself, "surely I can give it up."

Still, she could not forget how much she would have loved to own it. And it really was hers.

Hours passed bringing a keen sense of loneliness to Nancy. She wasn't having much fun—this sort of life, although it included so much that she could not have had at home, also lacked much that she would have had.

Romping about freely with her girl friends in the little summer colonies, doing unusual things, some of which had turned out wonderfully important for mere girls to accomplish, and, above all, that surrounding of loved ones—these were the things and conditions that Nancy missed.

Not that she didn't love Rosa, for she really did, but because Rosa was so very hard to understand, and was apt to do almost anything reckless, foolish and even risky.

Pitying herself a little, Nancy gave in to her homesickness. She refused to go over to Durand's with Rosa after dinner, she refused to take a walk with the suspecting Margot, who must have understood the signs she could not have helped noticing about Nancy, she even refused to listen to the radio, and decided to go to her own room—and read.

Passing Rosa's room she saw the precious blue cape thrown carelessly over a chair. The sight of it brought on a new fit of bitterness, and she dashed into the room, grabbed up the cape, hugged it, as if it were her own, then threw it swiftly over her shoulders.

There was no one in that part of the house. Rosa had gone over to Durand's and Nancy felt free to indulge in the coveted joy.

It was lovely! She stood under the big soft lights and gazed in the broad mirror, spellbound.

"It's mine," she whispered, "and I'll always make believe I'm wearing it."

Then came the test—Ted's test.

Glad or sorry? Was she honestly, truly glad or sorry that she had not told Rosa all that Betty had told her about the contents of that box?

Rosa felt so kindly now toward Betty, and Betty would have bought her any sort of a cape she had wished for, could she have only known!

Again she whirled around and hugged closer the soft, white fur collar.

Then she heard a step, a very light step, and turning quickly, she found herself facing Orilla Rigney!

CHAPTER XIV

THE SPY

The strange girl's vivid hair seemed ready to ignite, it was so blazingly red! Her eyes, a queer green, glared at the frightened Nancy, and altogether the intruder's attitude was one of defiance and challenge.

"Humph!" she sniffed. "So this is why you don't go out with Rosa; you like trying on her clothes when no one's around!"

Nancy flushed scarlet. So sudden had come the accusation, and perhaps because of her secret state of mind concerning the party cape, that she felt like one struck down by an enemy. Somehow the other girl seemed to tower above her, although Nancy was quite tall. The glare of those malicious green eyes seemed to take root in Nancy's own, and above all that red hair—yet Nancy had previously always loved red hair!

For some moments she did not attempt to reply to the cruel accusation. Then her defense flashed back, true to her instincts of high-born honesty.

"I have a perfect right to try on my cousin's things if I wish," she said loftily. "But what right have *you* here?"

"Keep your voice down," demanded the other in angry but subdued tones. "There's no need to get the house dogs after us."

"House dogs?"

"Yes, that old Margot—don't know why they didn't call her Magot," scolded the girl, "she's more like a watch dog than a woman. But I'm in a hurry. You needn't mind mentioning my call," she sneered, "and then, if I'm sure of that, I won't bother telling Rosa about your—party!"

The inference was so contemptible that Nancy shrank away instinctively. She had already carefully placed the innocent cape back on its chair, and was ready to lower the lights, but this last act she deferred. She felt safer with that high-strung creature under good, clear lights, at least.

But somehow as she looked at her, the subtle danger of Orilla's secret meetings with

Rosa flooded into Nancy's mind. For her, Nancy, to make an active enemy of Orilla would surely mean that much more danger to Rosa, whereas any possible compromise might at least insure Nancy some knowledge of the other girl's affairs.

She was thinking fast. Not that the term idealist (applied to her by Betty) in any way entered into her reasoning, but simply because she was Nancy of the disciplined mind, taught to think twice when in any serious predicament. And more than that, she had been cautioned by her mother, always to put down the proud spirit of revenge and in its place to plant courage. Courage to do that which was hardest, as it would invariably prove to be that which was best.

To understand Nancy as she was acting now, it is necessary to understand all this, although to her it was merely doing the thing that seemed best.

"Do you mean," she said very slowly, "that you do not want Rosa to know you have been here?"

"Yes," snapped the girl, "just like you

don't want her to know *you've* been here."

"But I don't care; why should I?" Nancy could not help that flare of defiance.

"You were trying on her new clothes, weren't you?"

"What's wrong about that?"

"Don't try to sneak, I'm in a hurry. Is it a bargain or isn't it?"

"What?" blurted Nancy, now a little bit frightened lest her chance to help Rosa might suddenly vanish.

"You keep your mouth shut and I'll do the same!"

The vulgarity of the girl's words offended Nancy's sense of respectable English, but she knew better than to show her resentment.

"But, did you bring a message or something?" she faltered. "Won't they know you have been here?"

"That's my business, you just 'tend to yours and don't worry about mine," snapped the stranger.

"It doesn't make any difference to me, of course, that you've been here — Orilla," Nancy almost choked on the name, but was determined to show some good feeling which she did not in the least feel—"and, if it suits you better, I don't see why I should tell Rosa."

"That's sporty!" exclaimed the girl, a complete change of her queer face, with its yellow skin and other peculiar colorings of hair and eyes, giving her a decidedly different expression. "No use being enemies, when we're both outsiders," she said next. "I must run along. Don't worry about party capes; they never make folks happy!" and she was gone.

Her last words, although almost whispered, left an unpleasant ring in Nancy's ears.

"Don't worry about party capes," she had said, almost as if she had discovered Nancy's secret. And then: "They don't make folks happy!"

Orilla seemed glad of that. Evidently she didn't want party capes or other luxuries, of which she herself had been deprived, to make folks happy.

Nancy moved cautiously. She felt as if she were still in danger—of what she could not guess. But since she had so inadvertently made an ally of Orilla, instead of an enemy, she knew she must be careful.

But was she now in league against Rosa? That is, of course, from an outside viewpoint. There could be no doubt of her action having sprung from the most honorable motives. She was doing a very distasteful thing, just to protect Rosa, if possible, from Orilla's secret influence. Yet, this would be hard to understand, and Nancy knew that it would be particularly hard for Rosa to understand.

"Well," she sighed to herself finally, as the last faint echo of that almost silent step had died away down the long hardwood hall, "we'll see what comes of it. But I didn't know what else to do."

She stood for a moment at the door of Rosa's room as she left it. It was a beautiful room; so much softness, such lovely silky things all about, and the glow of the bird's-eye maple furniture stood out even in that subdued light.

And yet—!

How empty it was! How it lacked personality! Even a certain untidiness which

Nancy always remembered as a part of Ted's humble little room was, after all, so personal, so Teddy-like!

The cape lay on the chair. It was a beautiful cape, but now instead of being merely beautiful to Nancy's critical eye, it was the symbol of something to be dreaded, to be careful about, and to hold as secret!

Just as she turned to enter the room which was now hers, Nancy pulled up sharply at the sound of another step.

"Is that you, Nancy?" It was Margot who put the question, and the sight of her was indeed welcome to the perturbed girl.

"Oh, yes, Margot," she replied, assuming as much ease as she could command, "I was getting a book from Rosa's room. I'm going to spend a whole evening reading."

The woman, who was more than a maid yet less than a relative, laid her white hand upon Nancy's arm.

"You will never regret having a fondness for reading," she said seriously. "There is nothing better for a young girl than a good book."

"Oh, I've always loved to read," replied

Nancy, flushing under the compliment, "but I'm afraid I like it too much. There are so many other things to do, you know."

"Of course, there are other things to do," admitted Margot, sort of leading Nancy into her room while she talked, "but I do believe in lots of reading. I can't get Rosalind to read anything but the most absurd stuff," her voice was full of regret at this point. "Can you imagine her reading boys' books? And detective stories?"

"Oh, yes," defended Nancy, "I know lots of girls who do that. And boys' books are good reading, sometimes." She feared each new sentence from Margot would be a question about the intruder, and hardly knew what she herself was saying.

"But you see, my dear, it's this way with Rosa. Let's sit down. I've been wanting a few minutes' talk with you."

Nancy pulled out a comfortable chair into which the portly Margot deposited herself. A low boudoir chair, the sort with the lovely square boxy arms, suited Nancy best and she placed herself into that.

"Rosalind is still a darling baby," went on Margot. "Because her own dear mother had to leave her when Rosalind was so young, I suppose I am a little too easy with the child, but you couldn't understand how very hard it is for me to be severe when I remember that poor dear mother."

Margot was surely genuine in her sympathy, and as she talked Nancy felt that she could understand. So that must be why Rosa had always, or almost always, conquered Margot, in spite of her usual talk to the contrary.

"She's not half as rebellious as she pretends to be," Margot continued, "but I have some worries." She stopped and looked so keenly at Nancy that the girl felt uncomfortable under the scrutiny. Then she suddenly asked:

"Has she told you anything of this girl, Orilla?"

"No, that is, nothing much," truthfully answered Nancy. "Mother has told me about Orilla's disappointment in having to leave Uncle Frederic's home," she added, thoughtfully.

"Well," sighed the trusted woman, getting

up and preparing to leave, "I don't mean to ask you to spy on your cousin, but I should be glad if you will do what you can to keep her away from that girl."

"I certainly intend to do that," declared Nancy, hardly recognizing her own voice.

"That's right, dear, and you won't be sorry. This is sure to be a trying summer, with Mr. and Mrs. Fred in Europe, and I'm so glad that you are here. Rosa needs companionship. No girl can grow up alone and be healthy, mentally. To be sure, she has had her school friends, but you see, my dear," again the deep sounding sigh, "it has been rather hard for her to make friends. She's so sensitive about her size. Why, one girl at school last year just followed Rosa around, she was so fond of her. But the child just thought she was seeking favors."

Margot, with this confidence and her apparent love for Rosa, had suddenly taken a new hold on Nancy's affections. After all, it is a woman a girl needs, Nancy was determining, and to her at that very moment—Margot was the woman.

CHAPTER XV

MYSTERIOUS HAPPENINGS

"I'll be sound asleep," Nancy decided, when she was finally settled in bed after spending a fitful hour trying to read. "It's the only way. I never could talk to Rosa to-night. To-morrow things will seem different."

Assuming her most restful attitude—lying flat on her back with her face "boldly turned up to Heaven," as Ted called Nancy's way of wooing sleep, she tried to think calmly.

"But what did Orilla want to steal in for?" persisted that question. "And even if she didn't want Margot to know that she came, why should she want to deceive Rosa?

"But somehow I don't believe she's as fierce as I thought she was at first," continued Nancy's reasoning. "She's sort of a bluffer, for she looked frightened when I defied her."

"Still, I believe it's better not to have her

for an enemy. She has sort of a catty look in her green eyes, and cats are terribly sneaky creatures."

Thus her thoughts hovered, like a balancing scale, for her encounter with the strange girl had been too exciting to be very soon forgotten.

"And if Rosa finds out without fully understanding!"

That thought was the most difficult to argue against, for the whole party cape episode had now assumed the proportions of real trouble.

"And yet it has made Rosa think kindly of Betty! Surely that is the most important thing of all," decided Nancy finally.

Trying to adjust all the other tangled ends into this silken tassel of beauty, she lay there, defying the ceiling to fall in her face, as the constant thought of little brother Ted had so often warned her it was sure to do, some night, if she didn't seek discreet refuge in the kindly bed clothes.

Yes, it would be lovely for everyone, especially for dear Uncle Frederic, if Rosa would become reconciled to the stepmother. Uncle Frederic loved Betty and Betty had loved Rosa's own mother; why, therefore, could not Rosa try to be grateful instead of rebellious?

Then it occurred to Nancy that Rosa was staying out rather late. Even being over to Durand's did not seem to warrant this late home-coming.

Night has a queer influence upon thought, and even a girl like Nancy, always brave and courageous when on her feet, could feel rather timid about things lying there in the dark, and staring at the ceiling.

What if Orilla had lain in wait for Rosa and enticed her to go away or something? What if Orilla had demanded money from Rosa? Would Orilla steal? That house had been the girl's home and it was not strange that she should sometimes want to visit it, came a more reasonable suggestion. And surely she would not steal, was the answer to that question.

But Nancy could not feign slumber, for her mind was too active to forget that the light patch above her was the ceiling, and not a bird's downy wing, bringing sleep, as the poets warrant.

Where was her mother now? So far across the sea that even the time there was not the same as that which ticked away patiently on Nancy's dresser. But her mother would surely enjoy the visit to those famous shrines of knowledge, for Nancy's mother loved to learn.

That darling mother! So pretty, so sweet, so kind and always so helpful! A deep, audible sigh escaped the girl on the bed as she indulged in this deliberation. Her mother had always been so like a girl chum, so companionable and such a refuge in trouble.

"But I shouldn't lean on her," came the accusing thought. "If I cannot rely upon myself, then mother's teaching would not have been well learned."

Following that came the thoughts of industrious little Miss Manners—Manny to Nancy and Ted. Then all the girl friends, who this summer seemed so far away, paraded before

Nancy's fancy, as they had so often done in reality.

A slammed door rudely broke up the soliloquy.

"Rosa!" exclaimed Nancy gladly, although Rosa was not yet in sight. "I'm so glad she's home safe!"

The relief was so great that Nancy promptly turned over and feigned sleep. She really couldn't talk to Rosa to-night, and she was sure her cousin would be just bubbling over with the evening's news.

A step in the hall, a halting at the door and then the whispered call:

"Nancy!"

"Yes," replied Nancy promptly, recognizing something unusual in Rosa's voice.

"Awake?"

"Yes."

"Then turn on the light."

"What's the matter?"

"Nothing."

"But you act so—so—" Nancy switched on the bedisde light.

"I'm just sort—of—out of breath."

"Been running?"

"A little."

"Why?"

"Silly, I guess."

"But what made you run, Rosa? You haven't a puff in you."

"I know. But my puffs give out easily." Rosa had sunk into the nearest chair and was breathing uncomfortably.

"But why? Did something frighten you?" pressed Nancy.

"Why—I was at the very door, Dell and Gar came to the very threshold with me, and then—oh, dear, what makes me puff so?" Rosa was still very much "out of breath."

"What was at the door?" questioned Nancy. She felt a little guilty in her relentlessness.

"Nothing. I was just opening it when I thought—I thought I heard a kitten. And I perfectly hate to leave a little baby kitten crying—all—night. Don't you?" Rosa managed to ask.

"Oh, of course I do," replied Nancy irritably. "But why should a crying kitten scare you?"

"It—didn't."

"What was it, then? For mercy sakes! You've got me all worked up," declared Nancy, who by now was out of bed and standing in front of Rosa's chair.

"That's just how I am; all worked up, so please don't make me any worse. In the language of the poets, I'm 'all—in!' "

"Of course, if you don't want to tell me," and Nancy turned back toward her bed, sullenly.

"But I do want to tell you; I'm just dying to, if you'll only give me a chance. Nancy, you know you are horribly impatient. We can't all be firecrackers like you." Rosa was recovering her breath, her spirits and her use of language.

"What happened?"

"Nothing. But when I thought I heard the kitten I crawled very carefully around to the side porch. You know how kittens can scat. And the porch was dark as pitch, so," Rosa was drawing out the story with provoking detail, "so, I called kitty, kitty, kitty! And I waited and listened. No kitty meowed an answer, and I was just turning back to the door when—something crashed down on the porch! Didn't you hear it?"

"No; what was it?"

"Betty's prettiest fernery, the white enameled one decorated with butterflies and flowers. Dad bought it for her when she came up here—a—bride!" There was tragedy in Rosa's tones.

"But you must have knocked it over," argued Nancy, none too sure of her assertion.

"I didn't! I couldn't have! I was nowhere near it!"

"Then who—could—have?" faltered Nancy.

"Someone who—wanted to spite Betty," Rosa almost whispered this, and still seemed rather shaken from her fright.

"I should suppose everyone in this house would understand his or her duty to Betty," insisted Nancy. "I guess that tall little stand went over in the wind, Rosa. You know what gales can shoot up from the lake. Have a nice time at Durand's?"

"Lov-ell-ly, but they mourned over *you* not coming. You have stolen Gar's heart from me, I'm afraid," teased Rosa. "He just kept saying nice things about you all the time. And we're going to the hotel to-morrow night. You can't imagine how excited I am—"

"Aren't you awfully late? Does Margot know you are out so late?"

"No, indeed. I phoned her hours ago and fixed it all up—"

"Rosa, I don't want to be preachy," interrupted Nancy, recalling poor Margot's serious appeal for her help, "but I can't see what fun you get out of fooling Margot. She thinks such heaps about you—"

"I know. She's a duck. But one has to have some fun, so I take—mine—this way," and Rosa swung herself about saucily. "Not that I blame you, little Coz, for trying to reform me. It's right good of you," and she flicked a kiss on Nancy's cheek as she prepared to take herself off.

Nancy was eager to do something definite, and she knew that Rosa's present mood was not too often displayed. Therefore she risked a straight appeal to the other's honor.

"Don't you think we ought to pledge ourselves to be truthful at least, while your father is away?"

"Truthful?"

"Yes. Not to deceive each other or Margot or anyone who has a right to our—our confidence," finished Nancy, rather laboriously.

Rosa sighed. "That would be awfully hard to carry out," she said. "For me, at least."

"Why?" demanded Nancy.

"Oh, I just can't tell you at this hour. Let's go to bed and dream of—to-morrow night's dance."

"All right, Rosa," assented Nancy, "but you have no idea how scary it is here when you are out too late. I can well imagine how Margot feels. It's really very strange to me, for you are awfully young to be so—so—"

"Sporty!" lisped Rosa rather comically.

"No, not that," Nancy scoffed. "We're

nothing but school girls, and I'm no good at pretending I'm grown up. But anyhow, Rosa, I hope *you* won't worry me to death!"

In answer to that the cousins reverted to the true girlship they were discussing, for Rosa fell upon Nancy's bed, and the way they talked, and the things they talked of, proved them girls, no more nor less.

CHAPTER XVI

DOOMED TO DISASTER

How that next day went by Nancy never knew. It seemed made up of moments, minutes, hours, and then a day of such confusion!

First thing in the morning there was general excitement over the breaking of the beautiful fernery. It had been one of Lady Betty's pet pieces, and one of her bridal gifts. Also, Margot herself had tended and coaxed the beautiful ferns and flowers in the long, narrow basket to their fullest perfection, so that Margot felt a sense of personal loss in its destruction.

And it had really been destroyed; not only knocked over and broken, but the fine enameled pottery was completely demolished, and the beautiful growing stuff crushed to a pulp!

No prowling dog could have been so thorough in its work, everyone said, but only

Nancy knew who had been prowling about, and only Nancy knew who, that very evening, had said things against the luxuries of the rich. And the fernery was a luxury.

Already the secret, which had been so curiously thrust upon her, was bringing its bitter penalty to Nancy. She had acted from the highest and most honorable motives, and yet, that little intrigue with Orilla, secretly knowing that she had been not only on the premises but actually in the house, through the rooms—all this brought to Nancy a sense of guilt.

Then, the broken fernery! Was that a part of Orilla's depredation? Would she really destroy things in her dislike for the people of Fernlode? It was before lunch that Rosa, first intent upon a swim, suddenly changed her mind and without explanation ran off some place; where, Nancy didn't know.

"Back in a jiffy!" Rosa had called as she went as fast as her weight allowed, toward Gar's waiting car.

And she hadn't even invited Nancy to go along!

From that time until the lunch bell rang, Nancy could not entirely fight down her feelings.

"I don't have to be treated this way," she decided, "I can go to Manny at any time. Manny made me promise I would, if I were not happy here."

But, when Rosa came back just in time for lunch, and made her take a pretty new fan she had bought for the evening's dance, reasonably, Nancy had to excuse her.

The postponed swim was taken in the afternoon, Rosa going out to the big rock and perching herself like a nice, fat bird upon it, while Nancy spent most of her time practising diving from the long dock.

All along the banks of the summer colony young folks were enjoying the water sports, and Nancy quite forgot her new anxieties as she too indulged in the pleasant aquatic exercise.

Just once Rosa became confidential. She asked Nancy if she knew anything about reducing systems.

"Why?" laughed Nancy. "You are not going to try one, I hope."

"One!" exclaimed Rosa. "I've tried dozens of them. Want to see me do the twelve-pound roll?" and without waiting for any encouragement Rosa raced out of the water, ran up the little sandy road that led from a hill down to the water's edge, and then proceeded to roll!

"Oh, don't, Rosa!" yelled Nancy. "You might strike a rock!"

But Rosa was rolling on.

Down, down she came, gathering speed with every turn and adding to her peril with it.

"Oh, Rosa! Grab something!" yelled Nancy. "You'll hit your head on those rocks!"

"No—no—I won't," Rosa managed to eject, each little word puffing out like a small explosion.

"I'll stop you," offered Nancy, jumping out in the path of the whirlwind.

"No, don't! I must—go—all—the way!"

"But how silly! You're a cloud of dust

and—and—just see those rocks!" entreated Nancy.

Still Rosa kept on tumbling along, first down the very steep sand slope, and then over a sharp turn not intended to be used as a road. It was the end of the hill slope that twined in to the boat house, and the lakeside drive did not connect with this, as the lake and its drive were at right angles.

It was over that sharp edge of rocks that Rosa tumbled, then, with one more blind turn, her heavy little body splashed into the lake at least ten feet below!

"Oh, Rosa!"

Nancy's yell was one of terror, but she did not wait to hear its effect, for the next moment she too was over the dock and into the water, grappling with the stunned girl, who seemed prone to go under the water every time Nancy attempted to assist her.

"Put your hand on my shoulder," Nancy ordered, "but don't grab me. Rosa! Rosa! Can't you hear?"

Then, realizing that her cousin must indeed

be stunned, Nancy shouted lustily for help.

"Help! Help! At the landing!" she screamed, meanwhile getting hold of Rosa's little skirt and trying desperately to raise the girl to the surface of the water.

The moments were agonizing, but Nancy tried to keep up her courage, calling as she struggled. But there was very little hope for immediate response, since each estate encompassed a large strip of territory and the bathers were now scattered, in canoes, most of them following the sun to dry out, down near the big float.

Finally, Nancy heard the welcome sound of disturbed water, and then saw approaching the Fernlode dock, a small launch.

"This way! This way!" she yelled frantically, her own strength ebbing from her continued paddling to keep afloat, and grabbing for a better hold on Rosa, for the water off the big bank at the side of the dock was suddenly deep, and decidedly treacherous, real depth being necessary for boat landings.

The launch was now alongside.

"Oh, quickly, please!" begged Nancy. "I think she's stunned."

Then she saw that the boat was being run by Orilla! And she was, as usual, alone.

"Don't get so excited," snapped the girl. "I don't see what you're so scared of. She could wade out of there."

"But she hasn't spoken. Oh, Orilla, please get hold of her. I tell you she's—stunned!"

In spite of her seeming indifference, Orilla was leaning over the side of the launch, and with her help Nancy had managed to get Rosa to the surface. She opened her eyes, sputtered water from her mouth, gasped, gagged and gurgled as if she were almost choked with water. Holding to the low side of the launch, Nancy ordered and bossed like a real life saver, but Rosa, although now able to help herself, made little headway at doing so.

Orilla scolded and grumbled. She hadn't time for such foolishness, and a girl who couldn't get up on her own dock ought to drown—according to her.

"She's got to get into your boat," insisted

Nancy, "she can't climb to the dock."

"All right, then, get in," growled Orilla, "and be quick about it. I've got to hurry!"

"You always have," retorted Nancy, none too pleasantly. "It seems to me, you might try to be—human, once in a while."

"Good enough for *you* to talk," flung back the other girl. "But you don't know what you're talking about."

"Yes," Rosa managed to gurgle, "and it's all your fault, Orilla Rigney, I've never had any—any peace since—"

"Cut it!" yelled the red-haired girl, so sharply that even Nancy, who was on the end of the dock, turned suddenly to see the girl's face masked in rage.

Rosa was now in the launch, Nancy sat, exhausted, on the end of the dock, but Orilla, at the engine, looked so peculiarly excited that instinctively Nancy shouted:

"Wait! Don't—start!"

But the engine had picked up and that launch was steaming off, Rosa still apparently too stunned to protest, and Nancy was powerless!

"Where are *you* going?" Nancy shouted, quickly as she could recover from her surprise.

But no answer came back; nothing but the chug-chug of the engine, and the boat's daring cut through the water.

"Rosa!" yelled the distracted Nancy. "Come back—"

Rosa turned and waved a fluttering hand, not gayly but sort of resignedly. And Nancy knew that all she, herself, could do was to—wait!

Certainly Orilla was heading her boat across the narrow end of the lake, at which point the water was sucked up by any number of little land patches, hills and foothills of the mountains. To land in any one of these would mean almost complete seclusion—for the thick evergreens made tiny forests of the islands. It was among these little islands that Nancy watched, impotently, for the last speck of color that identified the launch.

"Oh, what shall I do!" she moaned aloud.

"Rosa is not fit to go off with that girl. And who can go after her?"

The memory of Mrs. Pixley's plight out on No Man's Land, the evening that Rosa and Nancy went to her rescue, now came back to Nancy, with Rosa placed in the same predicament.

"If she ever leaves her out there alone," she worried, this time without speaking aloud, "we may not be able to find the spot."

"Hello! What's the mermaid pondering—"

"Oh, Gar!" gasped Nancy, turning to find their friend almost beside her upon the dock. "That girl, Orilla, has gone off with Rosa. And Rosa had been stunned from a fall down the hill into the water."

"Seems to me, Nancy, you're pretty well stunned yourself," spoke up the boy. "You look all in."

"Don't mind me, please! But think, quickly! What can we do to get—Rosa!"

"What makes you so dreadfully worried?"

Then poor Nancy tried to explain what had happened. As she talked she did feel her own loss of strength, as Gar had said, she was almost exhausted herself.

"Don't worry," comforted the boy. "I'll get Paul and we'll race out in our launch. I guess Orilla Rigney can't beat the Whitecap and I guess she doesn't know any more about mushroom islands than I do. You want to come along, Nancy?"

"Oh, yes, I couldn't stand the anxiety of waiting," Nancy answered. "I'll get into dry things—"

"And I'll pull in here for you in a couple of jiffs," Gar assured her, offering her his hand as she left the dock by the shortest cut—the hill that had proved too much for Rosa's rolling exercise.

"Do you think I had better tell Margot?" Nancy asked, when they had reached the point where their paths divided.

"Oh, no, better not. You see, when we get Rosa and fetch her back she'll just think we have all been off for a sail."

And Nancy knew as he spoke, that here was another boy with a disposition very much like Ted's.

CHAPTER XVII

SCOUTING FOR THE TRUANTS

If Rosa had been rebellious and uncertain in her conduct, her friends Gar and Dell were just the opposite, it seemed to Nancy. Waiting now a few minutes for Gar to return with his motor boat, Nancy tried to keep down her anxieties by building her courage upon the assistance of Gar, and as he presently hailed her from the landing, she saw that his sister Dell was with him.

"Two heads are better than one," he said simply, as Nancy stepped into the launch.

"Don't worry," Dell remarked. "Gar and I know those islands, although we haven't had a chance to do any exploring lately."

"But why should Orilla do that?" questioned Nancy. "She knew perfectly well that Rosa had been exhausted in the water and was unfit for anything but rest."

"You can never ask why, where that creature is concerned," answered Dell. "She's the unaccountable. Doesn't do any real harm but—"

"How awful close she does come to it," put in Gar, who was tending the smoothly running little engine, as Nancy sat near by and watched.

"This lake turns up real waves, doesn't it?" she remarked when a sheet of spray swept their deck.

"You bet," answered Gar, blinking to clear his eyes of the mist.

"I hope it isn't going to storm," Nancy added, apprehensively.

"Not right away, at any rate," answered Dell. "And the islands aren't far away. Better swing left, Gar. Here comes the steamer from the Weirs."

The swell from the big steamer struck the Whitecap presently, giving its occupants such a merry ride, that only their present upset state of mind prevented them from keenly enjoying it. Even the excursionists, who waved frantically at them, received scant attention in return, for there was no denying their anxiety. They must find Rosa, and they must take her away from Orilla Rigney, no matter what else happened.

Purposely Dell Durand avoided criticizing Rosa to Nancy, but this consideration could not entirely prevent Nancy from expressing something of her own confused opinion.

"You never saw anything like it," she recalled. "No sooner had Rosa gotten into the boat than Orilla seemed to pounce upon that engine—"

"Like a beast upon its prey," finished Gar, as a boy would when such a chance for such an expression was so obviously offered.

"She should not be allowed to come over to our side of the lake at all," went on Dell. "She has no business there and our docks are private property."

"But the lake isn't," her brother reminded her.

"Try Crow's Nest first," suggested Dell.

"That's a little place and we can scout over it in no time."

"Think I better—blow?" Gar asked.

"No," said Nancy. "Can't tell what Orilla might do if she had time to do it."

"Right-o!"

With a soft swish through the water the boat glided into shore, with the engine turned off.

Silently the three landed. Gar found a stout young tree to throw his boat rope around and in accord, without the need of questions, each of them immediately faced the little wilderness in a different direction.

"We'll come together by the big pine—see, right on top of the hill," Dell suggested, pointing out the big sentinel pine that stood guard over Crow's Nest.

"Better take a good, strong club," Gar advised Nancy. "Wait, I see one," and he made his way through brambles and briars to procure the end of a young birch that had evidently been broken in a storm.

Nancy thanked him, and with the staff began to beat her path through the bushes.

They did not really expect to find the girls actually hidden in the underbrush, but Orilla's habits were said to be so unusual that the scouts were prepared to find her busy at almost any camping detail on the island, if indeed it was this island upon which she had landed.

"Do you know that she carries a hatchet in her car?" Nancy asked, when Dell had come near enough for conversation, "I can't see what she would want with such tools as that."

"Well, frankly, Nancy," Dell replied, "I wouldn't be surprised to hear that she carried a shotgun, for the reputation given her around here is as vague as it is mysterious. Everybody seems to have a different story about Orilla Rigney."

"Yet she's—industrious, and honest, I suppose," pressed Nancy.

"All of that—too industrious. She not only works herself but wants to make the whole world work with her. Perhaps she's a case of misdirected energy. You know, Nancy, they say nowadays that that's as bad as sheer laziness," explained the older girl.

Sounds from treetops or from thickets attracted their notice then, and conversation was suddenly discontinued. But no sign of human life rewarded the most careful scrutiny of the searchers.

"I don't see how they could be around here without making some noise," Dell remarked.

"Take—no—chances!" hissed Gar, striking a comical poise with his mountain stick held high above his head, and his free arm struck out at right angles. His attempt at humor was rewarded with a wan smile from Nancy, but Dell only waved her club threateningly.

"We've got a lot of ground to cover, you know, Gar," said Dell seriously, "and we mustn't forget there is no guarantee of continued fair weather."

"I'm going to yell," the boy suddenly announced. "Better take a chance on Rosa hearing us than leave it all to the big gray fox."

A series of mountain calls followed. They were varied, queer, weird, owlish and even funny, for Gar proved to be an expert in the art.

No answer came. Instead, the silence of the woods after its interruption seemed even deeper than before.

Nancy sighed aloud, Dell did not try very hard to hide her own impatience and Gar protested openly.

"If we find her this time I think we ought to lock her up," he said, not entirely in jest.

"I—am ashamed of her," admitted Nancy. "But she really didn't do this. She actually blamed Orilla for her tumble in the lake," she recalled.

"That's probably why," declared Gar, " the orang-utan is now getting even."

"Well, we'll just try the other side of the oaks," proposed Dell, "then, we had better try some place else."

The little island covered only a small strip of land, which was made an island by a blade of the lake water that cut it away from another strip of land. To explore the entire territory took but a short time, and now the scouting party were scurrying down the other side of the summit, looking for the truants along the water front at that point.

"Someone has been here lately," Gar declared, as he kicked over a small stone furnace. "This always was a favorite spot for campers, you know, Dell."

"Yes." She surveyed the charred stones. "But our campers haven't been here. That stuff is old."

"Don't you think we had better shout again?" suggested Nancy. "I'm afraid Margot will be scared to death, although I did call something to her about going to the Point."

"Doesn't it beat the chickens!" murmured Gar. "Just imagine us hunting for those girls like a couple of lost—kids. Makes me think of our picnics long ago when *I* was the star for getting lost."

"You were clever that way, boy," replied his sister, "but please don't try it now."

"Oh, no," begged Nancy, frightened instantly. "Whatever would we do if you—got lost?"

"Don't worry, I won't. No fun in it without ice cream cones. But there's nary a one on this safety isle. Let's get in the launch and skirt the edges of the whole place. We can't possibly beat down bushes on all these piles of rocks."

"Indeed we can't," Dell agreed. "But suppose they didn't come in here at all? And where could she have left the launch?"

"She could hide that almost any place along here, for the edge has a regular curtain of young trees," the brother answered. "Nancy, don't look so dejected. When we find your cousin, maybe we shall find she has gone down to the ideal weight. I believe that's the main issue with poor old Rosalind."

"If we don't find her in any more trouble," Nancy replied. "But I'm never sure about her when she dashes off with Orilla. This is about the third or fourth escapade she has starred in since I came to Craggy Bluff."

"I couldn't count all she has starred in since I came up," Gar said dryly, as he untied the boat. The girls quickly stepped in and he promptly started up the willing engine.

Each new move in their expedition only brought greater anxiety to Nancy, for in spite of her companions' insistent attempts at gaiety, she, as well as they, felt that the finding of Rosa was by no means assured.

And it was so lonely, away out there, with shadows closing in from the sky, from the mountains and from the heavy growth of all sorts of trees, high and low, leafy and stark, in their pretty covering of silken foliage, or in their defiant armor of pine needles!

But nothing seemed beautiful; everything seemed sinister, and even the lapping of the waves against the rocks now struck terror into Nancy's heart.

Vacation? She had forgotten the word. Pleasure seemed very far away, if not entirely beyond her reach. All she thought of, all she wanted, was to find the unfortunate Rosalind.

"I'll swing in here and let's try that comic opera again," said Gar, determined to keep up their courage.

"The opera" was made up of the shouts

and calls, such as they had been practising ever since they decided to break the woodland silence, and following Gar's advice they again took up the refrain.

"There's a few birds answering, at any rate," Dell remarked, "but for my part, I think even the angels must have heard that yell of yours, Gar. If those girls are in these woodlands they either do not want to reply or—"

"There's the boat!" exclaimed Nancy, jumping up so suddenly she all but fell over in the launch. "I see it in that little clump of willows! Steer in there, Gar. They can't be far away from their boat."

And only too willingly did Garfield Durand comply with that eager request.

CHAPTER XVIII

THE WOODCHOPPERS

Under the willows, almost hidden in the vine-like foliage, they found the small motor boat that Orilla was in the habit of using. It was not her own, but belonged to a summer place that had not been opened for a few years past, and the owners were allowing Orilla to use the boat in return for some small care she gave to special plants upon the grounds and surroundings.

"That's the boat, all right," Gar announced, as he shoved alongside. "And just look at the—timber!"

The timber consisted of small trees, newly cut into pole lengths and placed into the launch, evidently ready to be carried off.

"That's queer," remarked Dell. "What can she want those for?"

"Not for wood," Nancy replied. "That

would stay green all winter. But let's hurry and hunt. Shall we call now?"

"Here's their path," replied Gar, instead of answering. "See how fresh the broken weeds are. Let's follow this a—ways."

Nancy's heart was fairly jumping with excitement. She did not want to guess at how they might find Rosa; whether she would be lying sick in that dark, damp woods, or—

"Hello there!" came a sharp call. "Meet Miss Robinson Crusoe—"

"Rosa!" exclaimed Nancy. "Oh, Rosa!" She couldn't seem to say anything else just then, the sight of Rosa was such a relief.

"Rosalind Fernell!" was Dell's emphatic greeting.

"Runaway Rosie," chuckled Gar, his stout stick beating viciously at the greenery that choked the little pathway.

By this time Rosa was in full view, and the searchers beheld her lugging great bundles of young saplings, her arms scratched and torn from her efforts to carry more of the poles than she could properly manage.

"Why the woodyard?" asked Gar, laconically.

"They're for Orilla—"

"Any objections?" demanded the girl just spoken of. She also was now visible, having come through a mass of clotted hazel nut trees, and she too looked like a picture from some foreign land, where women do all the chores.

"Yes, we have objections, Orilla Rigney," spoke up Dell, sharply, "and you ought to know well enough what they are."

"Let's help them load their boat," interposed Nancy, fearful that the unpleasant discussion would develop into something more serious. "Here, Rosa, I'll take some of those—"

"Do—please," murmured Rosa, her voice now betraying what Nancy feared—exhaustion. "I'm almost dead," she whispered, as the defiant Orilla made her way down to the boat. "I was never so frightened in—my life!"

"Neither was I," returned Nancy. "I'm shaking yet. What ever got into her—"

"Hush! She's excited and ugly—"

"What ever—"

"Let me lug those logs if you must have them," called out Gar, in his roughly frank, boyish way. "Goin' to start a new cure, Orilla? Is this tree bark good for snake bites or something?"

"What I'm going to start is my own business," snapped back Orilla, throwing her vivid head up high and bracing her thin body to carry the heavy load of wood. She was wearing a khaki suit, like a uniform, but even this, strong as the material must have been, showed more than one jagged tear from violent contact with the young trees, which must have struggled bravely against her cruel little ax.

"Have it your own way," drawled Gar, good-naturedly. "Here, Nancy and Rosa, let's help you. Maybe you're not quite so fussy."

Willingly enough Nancy and Rosa relinquished the rough sticks, their hands smarting and red from trying to tote them down to the water's edge.

No one said much, everyone seemed to realize that that was the only way to avoid trouble, for Orilla seemed ready to snap at every word, and the thing to do, obviously, was to get in their boats and sail away from Mushroom Islands, promptly.

"But it's all too silly," grumbled Dell aside to her own friends. "Why should we humor that girl?"

"We are almost ready to go now," Rosa coaxed. "And it is so killing hard to chop down those trees. Just look at my poor hands!"

The poor hands represented a pitiable sight indeed, for being pudgy and fat, they were easily bruised and torn, so that their surface now looked like nothing other than bruises and scratches.

Unwillingly they went back once more to the little woodland, where the devastation had been perpetrated, and there they gathered up what remained of the felled trees.

"You must have worked hard, Rosa," Gar commented. "Why don't you go in the business? Put a sign out, 'Woodlands Cleared While You Wait.' I tell you, I tried once on our back woods and didn't do anything like as well as this—"

To which Rosa did not risk a reply, for the quarrelsome Orilla was at her elbow directing the gleaning in no uncertain tones.

But it was not so easy to suppress Gar. He wasn't afraid of Orilla Rigney, and he was willing to let folks know it.

"Now, that's enough," he decided sharply. "We're not going to take another stick. If you want to chop down trees, Orilla, why don't you hire help? Or why don't you choose a woods nearer civilization?"

"What are you grumbling about?" retorted Orilla, letting drop more than one of the sticks she had just picked up. "I didn't ask your help, and I don't want it—"

"But there's a storm coming, Orilla," said Nancy very kindly, as kindly as she might have spoken to some troublesome child, "and we had better all hurry back. There now, it's all cleared up. Here, give me that long one. I haven't an armful this time."

So for the moment peace was restored, and the queer proceedings continued, until at last even Orilla seemed satisfied that the task had been properly finished.

Only to Nancy did she deign a pleasant look, and that look, Nancy thought, was rather secretive. For as the girl did half smile, she also winked one of her green, gimlet eyes, as if trying to convey to Nancy a message not meant for the others. This recalled the party cape episode, when Nancy compromised by agreeing, at least partly, not to mention Orilla's secret visit.

"But we found you, Rosa, at any rate," Nancy repeated, as again they paired off. "I'll never be able to tell you how I felt," she continued, giving the truant cousin a reassuring pinch.

Rosa rolled her eyes meaningly. "If you hadn't—" She left that contingency to Nancy's over-worked imagination, and again turned to help Orilla.

"Don't bother; just go along," ordered Orilla rudely.

"But aren't you going too?" Rosa questioned in surprise.

"Seems to me folks are awfully worried about what *I'm* going to do," snapped Orilla. "But if you'll all go along and take your pet with you—"

"Orilla Rigney!" called out Dell authoritatively. "What is the matter with you? Are you determined to make enemies of even those who are trying to help you?"

Nancy turned quickly to interpose, and as she caught a queer expression on Orilla's face she hurried to answer Dell before the other could do so.

"Now, Dell, please don't be cross," begged Nancy with a sly glance intended for Dell alone. "We had all best be going if we hope to escape that storm. Just see those clouds!"

"All aboard!" called out Gar. "Orilla, can't I push your boat out for you?"

"No, thank you. I'm not ready yet."

"But the storm," pleaded Nancy.

"I'm not afraid of storms. I love them."

"Out here, all alone?"

"I have birds and all the wild life of the woods. They are the friends I can depend upon," replied Orilla. And as she said this her voice was soft, pleasant, actually musical. It was plain where her affections lay.

"All right. Sorry. Hop in, girls. I'm heading straight for the other shore," Gar made known, starting up the engine as he talked.

Reluctantly they turned away from the solitary figure on the shore. She looked like a creature of the woods, indeed, the brown outline of her form merging so completely into the shadows, that it was scarcely distinguishable as the watchers swung around the end of the island.

"Why won't she come?" queried Nancy anxiously.

"Because she won't let us see where she goes," replied Rosa.

"And don't you know?" pressed Nancy further.

"No. She had promised to take me this afternoon—but—oh, well—" sighed Rosa. "I'm glad you came and I don't care much about her promises now. I guess I've been pretty—foolish."

"Only guess so?" put in Dell, in a way naturally expected from her, as the oldest member of the party. "We've been *sure* of that all summer. Just imagine, cutting down trees and doing that silly stuff!"

"Now, Dell," objected Rosa, a little huffed, "you must know I did have *some* reason. I'm not altogether a simpleton, I hope."

"So do we—hope," flung back Gar over his shoulder. "But there's a boat I've got to tow in. See them waving? Hold tight; I've got to turn sharp and these waves are pretty frisky."

All hands now turned their attention to the fisherman's boat, a little rowboat, quite helpless against the fury into which the lake was working its surface. It took but a very short time to reach the craft, then a man flung Gar a line which the boy pulled up until he could tie it securely into the stern lock of the Whitecap.

"Why, there's Pixley!" shouted Rosa. "See her trying to hold on to the fish. She's sitting in the bottom of the boat."

And those who looked saw the little woman just as Rosa said, trying desperately to keep her cargo from being washed overboard.

As she recognized the party in the Whitecap, however, she managed to shout her delight, for it appears she and her pilot had been battling the waves for some time before the launch came along.

"Ought to call you girls life-savers," she called out. "This is the second time you have saved mine."

"Maybe the third," joked Nancy to Rosa, "for if I hadn't saved her from the mob in the train when that grape juice bottle exploded—"

But Nancy just then saw a speck of light, like a spark, over in one of the group of islands from which they had lately embarked.

And it couldn't have been lightning, for the storm, though imminent, had not yet broken and there was no rumble of thunder even in the distance.

She looked again, made sure of the spot, but said nothing to her companions. The appeal Orilla had silently given her, with that glance from her deep-set eyes, seemed to Nancy too pathetic to be made light of. And perhaps the spark of light in the woodland, away out there where nothing but low, scrubby pine trees grew, had something to do with Orilla's secret. At any rate this was no time to discuss it. Confusion forbade.

"We'll be in before it hits us," called Gar gayly, surveying the racing storm clouds.

"And a good thing for us," added his sister, "for even this launch is not altogether safe in a real lake hurricane."

CHAPTER XIX

QUEER CONFIDENCE

When the excitement died down, and Nancy found an opportunity to "look Rosa over," as she expressed her scrutiny of the cousin's physical condition, she found so many cuts, scratches, bruises and other marks of violence, that she really wanted to call Margot in to attend to their cleansing and bandaging.

"I tell you, Nance, they're all right," insisted Rosa rather petulantly. "I don't poison easily and those are all scratches from the trees and bushes."

"But just see that long cut on the side of your leg—"

"A wire, I guess it was a barbed wire—"

"That's always dangerous," interrupted Nancy. "The rust is one of the worst things. Rosa, how could you be so silly?" Nancy's patience was by no means abundant. She hated to see Rosa's skin torn that way; besides, she realized the danger of it.

"Nancy Brandon!" called out the cousin in a determined voice, "you have no idea what I went through. Orilla acted like a lunatic and I was honestly afraid of her. She seems quite fond of you—" there was sarcasm in this—"that is, she spoke of you as if you and she were pals. Just another one of her oddities, of course, so I let it go that way."

Here was Nancy's chance to tell Rosa why the girl considered her friendly. But the hot flush in her cheeks warned her. Besides, there was in Nancy's mind a new thought. It came when Orilla had smiled at her in the woods. Perhaps Nancy could help Orilla!

So the moment passed and the cousins continued to bathe and bind the scratches. Rosa's hands were cruelly torn and, as the girls talked, Rosa gave Nancy an inkling of the whole absurd plot.

"I never expected she would ask me to chop down trees, of course," explained Rosa. "She had always insisted that what I needed was hard work. She made fun of me for being soft, and I suppose that made me mad. At any rate, she promised that I would lose five pounds a week if I faithfully followed her advice."

"Five pounds a week?" repeated Nancy, increduously.

"Yes. And you see, if I lost twenty pounds in the month the folks are in Europe I would be quite—quite slender when they came back," and she smiled so prettily that Nancy wondered why she wanted to spoil those dimples with trimming off their scallops.

"And she was going to do all that—with violent exercise?" Nancy questioned in amazement.

"That and—starvation." Rosa uttered the last word tragically. "I didn't promise to starve but—now, Coz, haven't I been humble enough? You don't want to hear any more of the horrible details, do you?"

"Well, I'd like to know," continued Nancy cautiously, "why she wanted the trees cut down? What was she going to do with them?"

"That's just what I wanted to know, too," Rosa said in reply. "I knew for a long time that she had some secret scheme; you know the night I hurt my foot we saw that she had a hatchet in her car, but she has never told me what the real plan was. I've known Orilla since I was a baby, and I suppose I'm used to her ways, but I must say she is secretive. And sly! I couldn't find out the least thing, ever, that she didn't want me to know."

"Yes, I think she is like that," agreed Nancy, thereby dismissing for a time at least the mystery of the plot. "But what we have got to do now is to fix up her damages. Rosa, I do wish you would let Margot see that big scratch. I'm no good at nursing and I don't want to take the responsibility—"

"I'll be as beautiful as ever in a day or two—see if I don't," replied Rosa, making desperate efforts not to wince as she poured the disinfectant over her hands.

"But when Margot smells this drug store

she'll surely suspect," intimated Nancy, for, as she said, the disinfectants had made havoc with the atmosphere of Rosa's little dressing room, that adjoined her bath.

"I'm always getting cuts on my hands," replied Rosa. "All I have to do is to hide the rest of me. Margot is pretty busy now, you know. If she hadn't been she would have heard old Pixley's story. Can't that woman talk though?"

Nancy agreed that she could, and that led to further discussion of Mrs. Pixley, Orilla, Mrs. Rigney and some other folks that Nancy had recently become acquainted with.

This was to have been the evening of the dance at Sunset Hotel, but there was now no possibility of the girls attending it. Not only did Rosa's battered condition make it impossible, but a heavy summer storm had descended upon the mountains, and showed no indications of subsiding.

Rain, wind, thunder, lightning! The girls watched the great spectacle from a west window, and at times it seemed as if the heavens were splitting asunder. The lightning flashed in a solid sea of fire behind one great mountain, and this looked indeed as if the sky were rent and another world was breaking through.

Somehow the storm seemed a fitting finish for the turbulent day that Nancy and Rosa had just passed through, and as they watched the display in the heavens they worried about Orilla. Was she safely under shelter? Why did not her mother prevent her foolish work? And, Nancy secretly wondered, what had that little flash of light meant which she had seen flame up suddenly and then die out?

For days following this there was no sign of Orilla nor did any word from her come to Fernlode. But this was in no way unusual, rather was it regarded as a good thing for Rosa and Nancy.

Mrs. Rigney came around occasionally, Nancy noticed, and she was surprised to find her a woman of intelligence. She appeared to be on the best of terms with Margot and the other servants at Fernlode, and this seemed to be cause for greater wonderment that Orilla should be so antagonistic.

Rosa recovered quickly, as she had promised to, and she also "reformed." That is, she no longer kept secret trysts with the "fat-killer," as she now called Orilla, although Nancy knew that letters, messages, and even bundles addressed to Orilla went out very privately from Rosa's room.

The arrival of a lovely white scales for Rosa's bath room came as a surprise one day, but a letter from Lady Betty presently explained it.

Rosa was to take long walks with Nancy, as she had promised to do; she was also to follow some sensible advice in the matter of diet, and just to keep up her courage she was to watch the scales!

This plan, which was really the fulfillment of Nancy's written suggestion to Lady Betty, brought the dove of peace to Fernlode, in so far as Rosa's conduct was concerned. For in the first week of her trial of it she actually lost three and one half pounds.

"And no barked paws nor skinned shins," she gayly announced to everyone, including, of course, the Durands.

"I can't see why you didn't know that insistent exercise and cut-down rations was the real cure," argued Nancy, reasonably enough. "Even at grammar school, and in the lower grades, babes, fat dimply little ones, are walking miles to school and turning their backs on lollipops."

"But I hate to walk and I love lollipops," explained the shameless Rosa.

"And you loved the excitement of a woodland mystery?"

"Yes; I could just see myself in a movie cutting down trees and falling away into skeleton lines. It was romantic now, Nance, wasn't it, really?"

"Very. Especially when we brought you back on a tray. All carved up like a tatooed injun—"

They yelled at this, and Nancy was so relieved at Rosa's change of disposition that she,

Nancy, began to get fat! Just as Lady Betty had hoped!

Everything was so happy and cheerful; Rosa's friends came almost every afternoon and evening, numbers of them, girls and boys, and at last the summer had opened up into a real vacation for Nancy.

They finally went to a dance at Sunset Hotel, and Rosa wore the blue cape. It was a perfect evening and everyone was so happy that even the sight of the cape upon Rosa's shoulders failed to bring regret to Nancy. Four car loads of young folks from their summer homes paraded down the hillside road at nine o'clock. It seemed late to Nancy, but she knew better than to say so.

"The hotel children have the ball-room from eight until nine," Dell had explained, "then the young folks swarm in. Don't worry about being too young, Nancy. You look like a young lady in that stunning rig."

The "rig" was stunning, even Nancy conceded that, for it was a flame-colored chiffon robe that fell down straight from her shoulders, sleeveless, and with the fashionable high neck. Her dark hair set the flame color off beautifully, as did the glints of her dark eyes, and she really did look lovely. This costume was one of Lady Betty's presents.

Whether a girl was fourteen or nineteen no one could tell, for the bobbed heads were so much alike and so ineffably youthful, everyone looked very young indeed.

The hotel was fascinating to Nancy; its great posts and pillars flanked with baskets of growing vines, the spectacular lights set all over the ceilings, and the music!

It was a scene of gaiety such as Nancy had never before witnessed, and when Gar had danced with her and had then taken her out to the great porch to see the lake illuminations, Nancy Brandon felt like a girl in a dream. Summer life at a fashionable resort was to her like a page from a book, or a scene in a play.

"But I'd die if I had to stay at a hotel," Gar assured her as she commented upon the grandeur. "It's all right once in a while, but you would hate this artificial living as a regular diet."

Nancy agreed that she might, but she also expressed her interest in a sample like this. Rosa had a wonderful time also, the best part of it being the number of compliments she received.

"Wasn't she getting thin!"

The dance ended early for the Durand party, as Dell was a practical chaperon, and she insisted upon returning to the hills at a reasonable hour. But the memory of that first night stayed in Nancy's mind just as she remembered her own little party in the What-not Shop last year.

Only Ted and her mother had been there to make that first one really complete.

CHAPTER XX

A SMALL BROWN BAG

And Rosa was getting thin! In this simple, easy, pleasant way—just long walks, daily. That meant rain or shine and "long" meant all the way to the village, clear down to the post office, two miles each way. At first Rosa objected; she found her feet untrained for such tramps, but Nancy knew and insisted.

"Why not try *my* cure?" she urged. "It's not near as unpleasant as Orilla's."

"Very well," Rosa would sigh. "But you better tip off the scales. If they don't mark me low—"

"They will," Nancy promised, and of course they always did.

Gar proposed tennis. Rosa had never before played—"good reason why," she explained, but now she was anxious to try the splendid summer game.

"You look wonderful in your sport suit, Rosa," Nancy encouraged, "and out on the courts—"

"All right. Anything once, but don't expect me to fly up in the air after the ball, the way you do, Nance. I'm still something of a paper weight, you know."

So tennis was tried, successfully.

"I know what was the matter with you, Rosa," her cousin told her one afternoon after an especially enjoyable set with Paul and Gar, "you thought you were fat, and so you were self-conscious and miserable. Now you think you aren't very fat, and you're proud."

"I think I'm not! I am not, am I Nancy? Tell me quickly! End this 'crool' suspense—" and Rosa performed a wonderful stunt with tennis racket and ball, actually "flying" off her feet in a really creditable manner.

She was so happy! No one who has always been free from such an insistent worry as Rosa's had been, can actually understand the joy of hope that a few pounds less flesh can bring. The hand of that little white scale became a friend, an understanding friend, and every time it pointed to a figure Rosa held her breath.

But this did not solve the mystery built around Orilla. Rosa herself was as keenly interested in that as was Nancy, in spite of her rescue from any actual need of it. Bit by bit she confided in Nancy details of the queer bargain between her and Orilla. She had shared her allowance with her, who insisted she had a right to some of it anyway, and that she would not "make Rosa as thin as herself" if she didn't pay well for it.

"But what has she done with the money?" Nancy asked, after that admission.

"Oh, I don't know," replied Rosa, innocently. "You see, she had some big project in her mind and everything else she could get was supposed to go toward it."

One evening when Nancy was seeking a little solitude along the lake front, there to read again her latest letter from her mother and the latest "funny page" from Ted, she was startled by someone calling her name in a hushed, whispering voice.

"Who is it?" she asked, although quite certain of whom it would prove to be.

"I, Orilla," came the answer, as the girl stepped from behind the shrubbery into Nancy's path.

"Oh, how you frightened me!" Nancy exclaimed. "I was so intent upon—my own thoughts. How are you, Orilla? We haven't seen or heard of you in such a long time."

"Oh, I'm all right," replied the girl, who as usual wore the dingy suit of khaki, and a boy's soft hat upon her thick red hair. "I'm glad I met you here. I want to ask a favor of you."

"All right, Orilla," said Nancy sincerely, "I shall be glad to help you if I can."

"I believe you. You're different. Maybe it's because you're poor—"

Nancy smiled broadly at this, but Orilla did not appear to notice it. She motioned to a rustic seat and they both sat down. Nancy was curious and a little anxious, for Orilla, while assuming friendship, still had that queer, furtive look in her eyes, and her face was surely unnaturally flushed.

"Have you been working too hard, Orilla?" Nancy asked kindly. "You aren't strong and you shouldn't—"

"I'm strong as an ox," interrupted the girl. "That's because I live out doors. I was sick once, and since I cured myself no one has interfered with my ways."

This, thought Nancy, must be why Orilla's mother allowed her to do as she pleased. But even so, she surely might have saved her daughter from wood chopping!

"Yes, I only go indoors at night—I steal in. No one knows where I go," this meant much to Orilla, evidently. "But you're my friend and we both have a secret, so that's what I want to tell you."

Nancy was so surprised she merely listened, not venturing to interrupt with a single word. Orilla kept locking and unlocking her fingers in a nervous way, and she fidgeted in her seat even more nervously.

As if the secret so long waited for was about to burst over Nancy's head, like a cloud before a storm, she waited.

"Yes, I know I can trust you," Orilla continued after a pause. "You're what they call an idealist, aren't you?"

"No, I don't think I am," faltered Nancy. "Why should I be?"

"Because you're so square. I've read about girls like you. They always want everything just right, no tricks nor sneaking. I knew that night when you tried on that cape that you were doing something for Rosa."

"Why? How did you know?"

"You looked it. When a girl is sneaking she doesn't flare up and get mad the way you did," went on the surprising Orilla and Nancy knew better than to prolong the discussion by any arguments. She merely smiled and accepted the words as they were intended.

"And since then you've never told," Orilla declared, her features drawn and strained as she talked, and her eyes shifting. "You never told Rosa, for if you had she would have told me. What she knows the world knows," said Orilla, scornfully.

"But Rosa has never said anything against you, Orilla," spoke up Nancy. "I'm sure you ought to give her credit for that."

"There you go again. I told you you were an idealist. But that's all the better for me. I can trust you, too."

This sounded like trickery to Nancy, and she said so.

"But you are lots older than I am and you ought to have lots more sense," she pointed out. "I don't mind helping you, if it's something you can't do yourself, but I must be loyal to my own family," she insisted, firmly.

"It won't interfere with your family, don't worry," replied Orilla. "I just want you to take care of some money for me. That's not so hard to do, is it?"

"Money!" Nancy remembered what Rosa had said about that. "Why can't *you* take care of it?" she asked.

"Because I suspect that someone knows I've got it, and they're after it." Orilla was very calm and composed now, and Nancy noticed how quickly her moods changed. "It's in this little bag," Orilla continued, showing to Nancy a square, brown bag made of khaki, just like her suit. It was bulky and seemed to contain quite a lot of money—if it were all money.

"Well, if you just want me to take it for a few days I don't suppose there is any harm in that," reasoned Nancy. "But suppose someone stole it from me?"

"No one would around here, that is, not up in your rooms," replied Orilla. "Please take it, Nancy. It means an awful lot to me," and she laid the bag on Nancy's lap as she pleaded.

"All right. But don't hold me responsible. I'll do the best I can to take care of it, of course," Nancy assured her, "but if anything *does* happen—"

"It won't. Thank you for taking it, Nancy. Now I am free to—finish my work," and she stood up to leave.

"But, Orilla, you were going to tell me something else; your secret place, wasn't it?"

Nancy felt now she should know more about Orilla's business if she were going to act as her secret treasurer.

"Oh, I can't wait now, but meet me here to-morrow evening at this time, and then I'll tell you. Good-bye, I must go. Don't mention having seen me," and just as she had done before, Orilla slipped away, back of the bushes like a wild creature of the woods, indeed.

For a few minutes Nancy sat there, the brown bag lying in her lap, an unwelcome treasure.

"How queer!" she was thinking. "And most of this was Rosa's. But Rosa gave it to her, so it really is Orilla's now. Imagine my being her—cashier!" and a little laugh escaped from Nancy's lips.

The gentle splash of a canoe paddle told of Orilla's departure, and Nancy checked her thoughts to listen.

"She is certainly the oddest girl I have ever met," she reflected. "But I had no idea of becoming a chum of hers. What would Rosa say if she knew?"

This was not a pleasant consideration, but somehow Nancy knew she could serve even Rosa best by agreeing, partly, with Orilla, so her misgivings were presently quieted.

Having the bag of money was certainly a tangible link between her and Orilla, and already Nancy understood its significance.

"I'd love to tell Rosa," she pondered, "but if I did Orilla would not trust me further, and I know I must keep her confidence, for a while at least. Just now Rosa is getting along so splendidly," she told herself, "and she's so relieved from her worries, that it surely must be best to keep her out of Orilla's affairs."

The little brown bag assumed almost a live form as Nancy clutched it. How long had Orilla been saving all that money? Some of it was in bills—that was easily felt through the cloth—and much of it was in coin; the weight vouched for that.

However, it was all in Nancy's keeping now, and she tucked it under her scarf as she entered the house. Meeting Rosa in the hall,

Nancy then accepted the plan for an evening at Durand's.

"Anything easy for to-night," she replied to Rosa's suggestion. "I don't feel a bit like thinking—hard."

CHAPTER XXI

ENTANGLEMENTS

A week passed and still Nancy guarded the bag, but in that time had neither seen Orilla nor heard from her. The girl's promise to meet her at the lakeside, on the evening following that upon which she had imposed the trust upon Nancy, had not been kept. Nancy waited until dark, and even a little later than she felt comfortable, out there alone away from everyone, and at a considerable distance from the house; but Orilla did not come.

Nancy imagined many reasons for her failure to appear. Perhaps she had feared detection, as she had the person she suspected of being after her money. Or perhaps her mother was keeping watch. Mrs. Rigney had been around Fernlode almost daily in the past week, and more than once Nancy heard her talking to Margot, as if she were in distress.

Orilla's name was mentioned often, but Nancy knew nothing more than that.

Finally, it was Rosa who broke the spell. She burst in upon Nancy one morning before breakfast.

"Nancy!" she exclaimed, "I'm just worried to death about Orilla. There's a reason why, but I just can't explain, if you don't mind. You've been such a dear, I perfectly hate to go at things this way again," and Rosa's face bore out that statement. "But if you'll only trust me this once more—"

"Of course I trust you, Rosa—"

"I knew you would. Then don't worry about me this morning. I've just got to go off and find her—"

"I'll go with you."

"If you don't mind, dear, I'd rather go alone."

"But I want to go, Rosa. I'm interested in finding her. In fact, I've got a reason—"

"Really! Are we both having secrets about Orilla? That would be funny if we weren't so worried, wouldn't it? But, Nancy, please let *me* find her and then I'll tell *you* where she is. I hate to seem secretive but—well, I just have to this time."

Nancy was baffled. Rosa was so positive in wanting to go off alone. And she, Nancy, was just as anxious to get in touch with Orilla. Why shouldn't they both go together?

"Rosa," she began again, "I'd love to tell you my secret, but you see I promised Orilla—"

"So did I," interrupted Rosa, smiling in spite of herself. "And, *you* see, if we both went she would believe we both told."

This sounded reasonable and Nancy hesitated. Rosa saw her chance and pressed it further.

"I'll come back as quickly as I can," she promised, "and then you can go talk to her."

"But you haven't had breakfast—"

"Yes, I have. I couldn't rest. I got to fussing and I went downstairs before even Margot was around. Don't worry about me, Nancy love," begged Rosa, pressing her cousin's hand impulsively. "I'll take good care of myself this time, and I promise not to cut down a single tree."

"But you are not going on the lake alone?"

"No; a friend is going to take me in her motor boat."

"Not Dell, nor Gar?"

"No. But someone just as trustworthy. You know Katherine Walters you met last week at Durand's? She's a regular old sea captain on the lake, and runs a boat like one."

"I saw her out the other day, in a big green launch—"

"The Cucumber. That's her boat and that's the one we're going in."

"Who else is going?" asked Nancy. "Why couldn't I sit in the boat with Katherine—"

"If Orilla saw *you* along she would never believe me," persisted Rosa, a little disconsolately.

"Don't you think we are humoring her an awful lot, Rosa?" Nancy asked in a strained voice; she too was bothered.

"Well, I suppose *I* am; not you. But just this once. You see, Nancy, Orilla hasn't much in life and she expected such a lot."

"You're good to her, Rosa, perhaps too good. But I hope you're not making another mistake; you know how she influences you."

"She couldn't now, Coz. I'm not in need of her services. You see, my doctor is a resident. I have her with me all the time," and again she flung her arms affectionately around Nancy.

There seemed nothing to do but agree, so after many admonitions from Nancy and promises from Rosa, the latter started off. She had arranged things with Margot so as to allay her suspicions, and when Rosa waved to Nancy from the green launch, called the Cucumber, Nancy sighed in spite of the beautiful morning and all other favorable circumstances.

Hours dragged by slowly. First Nancy wrote letters—it would soon be time for home-comings—then she drew a pen and ink sketch for Ted. She even finished the little handkerchief she was hemstitching for Manny, but yet there remained a full half hour before lunch time. And no sign of Rosa!

It might have been that Nancy had not yet gotten over that anxious search for Rosa, when she and the Durands finally found her on Mushroom Island, at any rate, all that morning Nancy worried.

Lunch time came but Rosa did not. One, two, three o'clock! Nancy could stand it no longer. She made some excuse to Margot and hurried over to Durand's.

It happened that Paul was there, and, of course, Gar was with him; but Dell had gone out.

"Look for Rosa!" shouted Gar, just as she knew he would when she told why she had come. "Say, Nance, what is this, anyway? A bureau of missing persons?"

She explained without fully explaining, and the boys gladly enough set sail in the Whitecap, once more to search for the illusive Rosa.

"But no wood carving, wood chopping, nor wood lugging," declared Gar, gayly. Then he told Paul about his previous experience in that line, embellishing the story with extravagant little touches peculiar to the style of Garfield Durand.

Paul and Nancy, as usual, found many things to talk about, to discuss and even to disagree over, for Paul proclaimed the beauties of New Hampshire while Nancy held with unswerving loyalty to the glories of Massachusetts.

But her anxiety over the delay of Rosa's return was not even thinly covered by these assumed interests, and only Gar's continual threats to do something dreadful to the runaway "this time sure" and his repeated avowals that he positively, absolutely and unquestionably would not "dig up the woods nor chop down trees in this search," kept Nancy's real worry from being mentioned.

"We don't have to go on the islands to look for the Cucumber," Gar insisted. "The girls couldn't hide that boat if they tried. It's so green you can hear it, to say nothing of the noise that engine makes."

"Oh, no, we don't have to go inland at all," Nancy agreed with elaborate indifference.

"I just wanted to look around and hurry Rosa along. She has a way of staying over, if it's only to gather weeds. Rosa doesn't seem to worry, ever, about keeping her appointments, but I didn't want Margot to spoil any of our fun, just because Rosa stayed out all day, you see," finished Nancy, quite confused from the length of her speech and its utter improbability.

"Let's skirt around these islands," proposed Paul, "and if we don't spy the Cuke we better try over at the Point. They may be picnicing. Katherine loves the lollypops they sell at the Point—I know."

"All right," agreed Gar, "but after that I've got to get back. Promised to drive down for Dell, you know, and *she* isn't walking off fat."

They skirted the islands but did not discover the long green boat at any landing or out upon the lake. Then they proceeded to navigate in the direction of the Point. Here they encountered many boats of many descriptions, for the Point was not only a pretty point of land extending out into the water, but it was also a point of recreation and general interest for summer folk for miles around.

"Not here," reported Paul, for there was no sign of the girls, and the boat was nowhere to be seen. "Better go back home. They could have gone in through the cove, you know."

"Of course they could, and I'll bet they have," declared Gar. "Well, we had a fine sail, anyway. Hope *you* enjoyed it, Miss Brandon?" he finished in assumed formality.

"Very much," simpered Nancy imitating Gar's affectation. "I had been rather dull all day, but *this*—" she swept the lake with a broad gesture—"this is glorious."

"Joking aside," said Paul, "are you having any fun, Nancy? That cousin of yours is as hard to manage as a young colt, I'd say."

"Oh, no, she isn't, really," replied Nancy. "We have wonderful times now, much better than we did at first when we didn't understand each other."

"And you claim to understand Rosa now?" asked Gar, swerving his boat into the small cove that lay beside his own summer home and Fernlode.

"Well, yes, I think I do," spoke up Nancy. "But then, Rosa's my own cousin and that makes it easier."

"Maybe that's it," retorted Gar, "because I'm not so dreadfully stupid, I hope, yet I can't understand her a-tall."

"Now look!" cried Paul suddenly, standing up and pointing to Fernlode. "There they are! What did I tell you!"

"That," replied Gar, crisply, slowing down his engine.

"Oh, I'm so glad," breathed Nancy, in her joy betraying how anxious she had been. "But the boat is going off!"

"Yes, but your dear little Rosalind is all right, standing there all by her little self. See her?" said Gar, as usual teasing about Rosa.

It took but a few moments to pull up to the long landing, but the Cucumber had already steamed off and, as Gar had said, Rosa stood there, waiting alone.

One look at her cousin's face and Nancy knew she had been disappointed. She had not found Orilla.

CHAPTER XXII

A GIRL AND HER ROOM

Nancy found Rosa, as she suspected, disappointed and even worried.

"It was the strangest thing," Rosa explained, "every time we thought we had found Orilla she just seemed to disappear. Of course she didn't, but on the lake there are so many turns, and ins and outs and, being in the boat, we stayed on the water. I suppose Orilla was on land," she finished sullenly.

"Why was it so important for you to see her to-day?" Nancy asked, innocently enough.

"I had a message for her, and that should have reached her to-day," replied Rosa. But she did not go into details and Nancy felt that she could not question further. However, she did try to reassure Nancy that Orilla would probably be around before nightfall.

"I hope so," Rosa said, "if not, I simply

don't know what I shall do. I went to all her woodland haunts that *I* know of, and land knows she's got enough of them, but there wasn't even a trace to show that human footprints had been over the ground lately. Oh, dear, isn't it awful to be a crank? Orilla is just a crank, and I tell you I'm about sick of her ways," Rosa pouted. "But I have to get some of the loose ends tied up before I can wash my hands of it, as Margot would say."

"And there she is," Nancy reminded Rosa, for at that moment Margot was coming down the path at a brisk rate.

"On the war path," Rosa remarked. "I've got to surprise her with some news. Let me see! Oh, I'll tell her about a big sale of linens down at Daws," and forthwith Rosa rushed up the path to proclaim the glad tidings to the unsuspecting Margot—or the Margot who was pretending to be unsuspecting.

From that moment until after dinner and until almost nightfall, the cousins had not a moment to themselves, for company came, and Rosa had to entertain. Nancy also helped out, the visitors being most interested in her simple reports from the neighboring state. When they were leaving (they were the Drydens from the Weirs and were staying at a hotel in Craggy Bluff) Rosa drove in town with them to bring some mail to the post office, but Nancy declined to go. Rosa was to meet Dell Durand and drive back with her, and as Dell had talked to Nancy on the phone and assured her she would be back before dark (all this in coaxing Nancy to go), there seemed no danger of delay for Rosa.

When they had all gone Nancy felt herself free at last to take her favorite stroll along the lake front. The sunset was glorious; golds, purples, greens and ashes of roses, in hues too brilliant to be so tersely described. Is there anything which can beggar description as can a sunset on that great, majestic lake! Words cannot tell of it, no more than the mist can veil it.

"It looks as if heaven were leaking joy," thought Nancy, as she watched the descending beauty.

Thinking of her mother, of Ted and of dear Manny, as she did every evening, this being a part of her filial love and devotion, Nancy gazed and wondered, until suddenly a step near her startled her from her reverie.

It was Orilla!

"Oh!" exclaimed Nancy. "I didn't see you coming—"

"No, one can't. I have so many secret little paths around here," spoke Orilla, and Nancy noticed that her voice was very low, subdued, and her words rather well chosen.

"But I'm so glad you came," Nancy hurried to add. "We've been looking everywhere for you, all day."

"I've been away, to the city, and I'm so tired!" With a sigh she sank down upon the lake-side bench. "I believe I would die if I had to live in a city," she murmured.

"It is dreadfully stuffy after air like this," agreed Nancy. "But you are not sick, are you, Orilla?" she asked anxiously, for Orilla did seem very unlike herself.

"No, I guess not. I have an awful headache but—don't let us talk about sickness," Orilla broke off suddenly. "I have something more important to talk of to-night."

"First, Orilla," interrupted Nancy, "won't you please let me give you your little bag? It has worried me—"

"If you'll only keep it a few more days, Nancy—"

"But why? Shouldn't your mother take care of it for you?" questioned Nancy. She had been determined to get rid of the treasure and this was her chance.

"Mother?" Orilla's voice showed disapproval of that idea, most emphatically. "No, mother is good and has given me much freedom, but she doesn't quite understand me, you see, Nancy," finished the girl with one more of those weary, heavy sighs.

Before Nancy could speak again Orilla had risen and was leading the way to the other end of the spacious grounds.

"Come this way," she said. "We won't meet anybody and I must not delay too long."

"But Rosa may be along—"

"Let me tell you alone, Nancy, please," pleaded Orilla. "Then you may tell Rosa if you want to. I'm tired of secrets, tired of being hated and tired of fighting. Until you showed some friendliness for me, I haven't ever remembered kindness except from mother, and, well, just a few others," finished Orilla, evasively.

She was hurrying toward the rear of the big house and Nancy was following. The path she picked out was quite new to Nancy, who thought she had discovered every little nook and corner of the big summer place, but this was a mere strip of clearance, tunneled in under heavy wild grape vines that grew clamorously over high and low shrubbery, and even climbed into the biggest wild cherry tree.

Neither girl spoke for some minutes. Then Orilla asked Nancy if she liked Fernlode.

"Why, yes," Nancy replied, "I love it."

"So do I," declared Orilla sharply, "and you know they—put me out!"

"Oh, no, Orilla, they didn't do that," Nancy hurried to correct her. "When Uncle Frederic married—"

"I know all that, Nancy, but don't let's talk of it. It makes me furious, even now. Don't talk any more—some one might hear us. Just come quietly after me," she whispered.

Where could she be leading her, Nancy wondered? Surely this was the end of the house just back of the servant's dining room —

Orilla stepped up to the corner of the building, and then Nancy saw that they faced a small door. It was situated at the extreme end of the first floor and almost hidden in heavy shrubbery. While Nancy waited, Orilla surprised her still further by taking a key from her dress and turning it in the lock.

The door opened!

"Orilla!"

"Hush! Just keep close," whispered the girl. "It is only dark at the entrance."

By keeping close Nancy soon found herself in a quarter of Fernlode she had never before explored. She knew that it must be the servants' quarters, and before she could speculate further, Orilla had unlocked another door and they both found themselves in a pleasant little room!

"This is—my—room!"

Nancy could scarcely breathe, she was so frightened at the tone in which Orilla said that.

Her room!

"You see, these are all my things, and I come here whenever I get a chance," Orilla confessed. "No one ever thinks of looking in here, and I never take anything away. I wouldn't do that, you know," she said very positively, as if fearing Nancy's opinion.

"Your—room!" Nancy was too surprised to get past that unbelievable statement.

"Yes; and no one else cares for it or needs it." Orilla was straightening around the brown reed chairs and patting the small table cover, and as she touched a thing, her affectionate interest in it was plain even to Nancy's excited gaze.

"Doesn't Rosa know?" Nancy asked finally.

"No. Rosa has been away a lot, you know, and besides, the Fernells only come here in summer. I was born in these mountains, and as a child mother brought me here. She's a nurse, you know, and a wonderful mother." Orilla sat down and pointed out a chair to Nancy, which the latter gratefully accepted.

Nancy knew little about Mrs. Rigney, but she guessed now that probably her love for Orilla had led her into the mistake of allowing her daughter to grow up believing Fernlode to be her own home.

As if divining Nancy's thoughts, Orilla said almost that very thing.

"Mother was devoted to the real Mrs. Fernell," she said, thereby disputing Lady Betty's later claim, "and Mrs. Fernell was lovely to me. While Rosa was away at school I played around here as—well—you can imagine how I felt to be put out of *this* room!" she again challenged.

In vain did Nancy try to explain the situation, defending Lady Betty's purpose in keeping no one but servants on Fernlode, but

Orilla would not be convinced of its justice. Suddenly she threw herself upon the bed with such secret enjoyment, that Nancy knew the girl's mind had become morbid on the subject of ownership.

As so often happens with those who are physically delicate, her reasoning also was at fault. She imagined she had been unjustly treated, whereas nothing of the sort had happened. Mr. Fernell had been generous to the point of bounty in educating Orilla and in giving a sum of money to the mother. This had all been done because of Mrs. Rigney's devotion to Nancy's Aunt Katherine, the first Mrs. Fernell, and Nancy knew the story well.

"Yes," Orilla began again, "it was not mother's fault. And she has tried to make me see things her way; but I can't. I've always been a wild mountain girl and all that I've loved has been here. You don't think I did wrong to come back here once in a while, do you?" she asked plaintively.

Nancy gazed silently at the girl upon the bed. Her hair, always so fiery red, did not look quite so peculiar on that pillow—Orilla's own pillow, that she had so long loved. The room was musty and needed a thorough airing, but Nancy noticed a small casement window opened slightly—this was, she reasoned, Orilla's way of secretly ventilating the room.

"I don't see what could be very wrong about your coming here," Nancy finally answered Orilla's question. "But why didn't you ask?"

"Ask? After being turned away?"

"You were not turned away, Orilla, and that's a foolish thing to say. Uncle Frederic simply changed his plans and there was no need of a nurse here," stoutly and emphatically proclaimed Nancy.

"And they didn't like me to be with Rosa—"

"Now, Orilla, you can't deny you were not a suitable companion for Rosa, because you could make her do anything. You are older, and you worked on her sympathies," Nancy felt obliged to point out.

"I'll admit that now, Nancy, to you, but it didn't seem that way before. I never told anyone, not even mother, how I felt, and it just all piled up inside of me until I imagined myself like a volcano, always ready to—erupt."

This was the first time that Nancy had noticed any depth to Orilla's character, and she had continually wondered where the educational influences, said to have been provided by her uncle, had been hidden in the girl's personality. But the confession of her morbid, morose state of mind was plainly the answer. She had fought down culture, choosing to be simply a wild girl of the mountains.

"My mother always insists upon us talking things out," said Nancy quietly. "It's so much better to share our worries—"

"I know that now. I feel like a different girl, just from talking to you, and you're only a kid," said Orilla, again betraying her disregard of polite English. "I'm through with secrets, Nancy," she continued, jumping up suddenly from the bed, with evident nervousness. "One secret leads to another until I am fairly smothered in them. Now, this one is not so heavy, but there—are—more."

CHAPTER XXIII

SHEDDING SECRETS

Orilla was now moving about the room in such an excited manner that Nancy became alarmed!

"Come on out, Orilla," she begged. "I really have stayed too long. Rosa will be back—"

"All right. Let's go. But I want to tell you that I broke the fern stand—Mrs. Betty's, you know," Orilla said, her voice raising beyond the pitch of security. "I came back that night—mother was to be away a week and I came up here for that one night—and I had forgotten my key. I was so mad to have to go back home all alone and it was late, you know, that I just smashed that fancy stand for revenge!"

"Orilla! That lovely fernery!" gasped Nancy.

"Yes, I know it does seem cowardly," admitted the girl, "but my head was splitting—"

"You have a headache now," interrupted Nancy, noting again the girl's highly flushed face.

"Yes, and I must go," she cast a lingering look about the room, which really was quite cozy. "How I would love to be able to come in here and fix things up," she sighed.

Nancy was thinking of a possible plan, but she had no time to mention it now. She wanted to get outside and find Rosa.

"Of course I'm going to tell Rosa," she said, making sure of speaking positively so that Orilla would not expect to object.

"I suppose you can. I am so tired of secrets that I was determined to tell you before my old crankiness would come over me again," confessed Orilla. She had locked the door and again they were treading their way under the wild grape-vine tunnel. "I don't know why it is that some people can soothe one so. I should never have thought of confiding in anyone else, and yet you're just a little girl," reasoned Orilla wonderingly.

"Maybe that's it," replied Nancy brightly. "Because I'm little—"

"Oh, no. That isn't all of it, but you wouldn't care for soft soap," said Orilla wistfully.

"I'm sure I hear Rosa—"

"But I must go, Nancy. My head is bursting, and if I get talking to Rosa, she'll say so much—"

"You know she has been looking for you all day," persisted Nancy, anxiously.

"I can't help it. Everything has got to wait—until to-morrow. Tell her I'll be here in the morning—if I'm able—"

"Orilla, I can't let you go," interposed Nancy. "I'm afraid you're sick—"

"No, I'm not, really. I have these headaches often, and bringing you into my room, you see—"

"Yes, I understand," said Nancy kindly. "And if you feel that perhaps, as you say, you had better get quiet. All right; I'll tell Rosa.

Don't worry that she'll find fault; she always speaks well of you, Orilla."

"Yes, little Rosa's all right, but silly. She was so ashamed of being fat—why—" and a little laugh escaped Orilla's lips. "Wasn't she foolish?"

Nancy heard voices from the roadway just as Orilla slipped into her boat and paddled off. Finding the secret room had been such a sudden revelation that Nancy could scarcely understand it all even yet. That Orilla should have so loved that room, and that she had been coming to it secretly for so long a time, seemed incredible.

"Uncle Frederic would have let her have it, I'm sure," Nancy reasoned, "and *I'm* going to ask him to," she determined, when the unmistakable voice of Rosa floated in through the hedge.

It was going to be exciting, Nancy knew, this news to Rosa. It would surely be met with one of Rosa's typical outbursts, so she decided to postpone the telling until Rosa was safely, if not quietly, indoors.

"Drydens want us to come to their hotel some night," Rosa reported, "and we must go. Nancy, they think I'm thin enough. What do you think of that?" and Rosa took a look in the mirror to help Nancy's answer.

"Calm yourself, Rosa," said Nancy importantly. "I've got such news—"

"Orilla been here?"

"Yes—"

"And she's gone? Why didn't you chain her till I came—"

"I couldn't, Rosa, she had a dreadful headache—"

"Headache! What's that to the trouble I've got? Her troubles, I mean," and Rosa fell into a chair as if in despair.

"Do let me tell you, Rosa. I feel a little done up myself."

"Selfish me, as usual. Go ahead, Coz. I've got my fingers crossed and am gripping both arms of the chair. No, that's a physical impossibility; but I've got my feet crossed, so it's all the same. Now please—tell!"

"Did you have any idea that Orilla came to

her room here, in this house?" Nancy began in her direct way.

"Her room? In this house? What do you mean? She hasn't any room here!"

"I mean the room she had before Betty came—"

"That little first floor corner—"

"Yes, behind the storeroom, down by the west wing—"

"I knew there was a corner of the house there, but it's been shut up for ages," replied Rosa, already showing her eagerness to hear all of the story.

"Well, poor Orilla could never give up that room, and she has been coming to it every chance she got. She took me in there to-night and I never saw anything so pathetic," explained Nancy simply. "She fairly loves the room and insists that it should still be hers."

"Can you—beat—that!" Rosa was so surprised no other wording seemed strong enough for her. "Coming to that little cubby-hole!

Say, Nancy, honestly, do you think that Orilla's crazy?"

"No, I don't. But I've heard mother tell of such cases. And I've read about girls keeping their baby loves, old dolls, you know, and things like that. But this is the oddest—"

"For mercy sakes! How ever did she manage it?" Rosa asked, blinking hard to see through the surprising tale.

Then Nancy told her, as well as she could, how Orilla came by the elderberry path, from the lake, through the maze of wild grape vines to the small door of the small porch at the west end of the big rambling house.

"I always said," put in Rosa, "that there was a door for each servant around this house, but I must have missed that one. Well, poor old Orilla! I guess she's quite a wreck, isn't she?"

"She had a headache, as I told you, but she seemed glad to get rid of some of her secrets, and I don't wonder," admitted Nancy. "She has enough secrets to make a book. But I told her *I* wasn't going to keep any more of them. I told her I was going to tell *you* everything she told *me*."

"Goody for you!" chanted Rosa. "And go ahead—tell."

"Well, she asked me not to tell you when she had been here one night," began Nancy, taking another chair for a fresh start in the narrative. "I didn't then, as it couldn't make much difference—"

"She came sneaking in here—"

"She came through the hall the night the things came from Boston," went on Nancy. "And I might just as well tell you all about it."

"All?"

"Yes. I was standing right over there trying on the blue cape—"

"Nancy! You liked that cape!"

"Yes, but I like the red one—"

"You don't. I know now. That cape was intended for you and I'm a greedy thing to have grabbed it. Of course, *you* wouldn't even hint—"

Nancy was a little confused now. She had

never expected the blue cape issue to come up again. But Rosa was positive and would not listen to Nancy's protests.

"But, Rosa," Nancy insisted, "Betty said she would love to get things for you if you would only let her. And surely, when you admired the cape—"

"Oh, yes, I know. You being Nancy, and all that," said Rosa, meaningly. "Well, *I'll* forgive you. You did succeed in getting me to listen to reason and now I'll try to be civil to Betty."

"You would have been, anyhow," said Nancy. "Because you were bound to be more reasonable—"

"I'm not trying to compliment you, little dear, so don't try so desperately hard to shut me off. But all the same, look—look at my figger! Ain't it just grand!" and Rosa strutted again before the patient mirror making sure doubly sure that she was quite genteel.

"I suppose you'll think I'm complimenting you if I tell you how well you look," retorted

Nancy. "But I'm sure you have gone down twenty pounds!"

"And a half," flashed Rosa. "Twenty and one-half pounds less, and my clothes are falling off me. Won't dad and Betty howl?"

"But you've got to keep up your walking, your tennis and non-candy schedule," Nancy reminded her. "Don't forget that. All right, don't answer, please, I have heaps more to tell you about Orilla and we're miles off the track."

"My turn. I've got to tell now; you listen. First about the blue cape. You've got to have that. No, don't object," as Nancy seemed about to do so. "I feel like a thief now. To have taken that from you," declared Rosa.

"I wish you would keep it. Just to show Betty how you liked her choice," Nancy argued.

"I won't. I care more about your choice. Besides, I can wear something else she bought, so don't worry. But about Orilla. You said she had let down the bars on all secrets? That we can tell?"

"Yes, she agreed *I* could," replied Nancy.

"Then that's good enough for me," decided Rosa. "Now you sit pretty and listen, but don't faint. The reason I tried so desperately hard to find her to-day was because I had a message from Boston for her. Her fresh air kids are arriving to-morrow," said Rosa facetiously, drawing a funny face.

"Fresh air—children!" corrected Nancy. "What does that mean?"

"It means that the wily Orilla has made arrangements to entertain some poor children and their caretaker at a camp that she hasn't got. She thought she would have it—I suppose that was what I was chopping down trees for—but the camp doesn't seem to have developed. And those children leave Boston *early* in the morning!"

"Do you mean that Orilla agreed to take children at a camp out here and now they are coming—"

"Exactly. And the camp isn't. That's the little fix *I'm* in."

"You're in?"

"Yep. I got her mail and it came here in

my name. It didn't seem much to do for her, but I'd like to know how I'm going to forestall those children, who will leave their humble homes with their breakfasts in shoe boxes tomorrow morning."

Rosa's mood was happy and her expressions flippant, but for all that Nancy knew she intended no disrespect to the strange children.

"You mean they expect to come to Fernlode?" Nancy queried, puzzled anew.

"They seem to; although, land knows, I didn't expect them to. You see, Orilla couldn't give up the idea of this being her headquarters and I, poor dumb-bell, just helped her carry it along."

"Well, there's no harm done," said Nancy calmly.

"No harm done! Wait till I get you to read that telegram. There, read it and—rejoice!"

Nancy read the message. It stated that the children, a dozen of them, would arrive at Craggy Bluff on the morning train and directed the recipient of the message to be sure to meet them with cars!

"Oh," said Nancy. "That is rather complicated, isn't it, for it's addressed to you?"

"Bet your life it is," flashed Rosa. "And please tell me quickly, pretty maiden, and all that, what's a girl to do about it?"

"You don't suppose Orilla has the camp ready?"

"I know she hasn't. She sent message after message, or I did for her, to keep them back. But now they're coming to-morrow!"

"Then, let them come, that's all," said Nancy.

"Yes, just like that," Rosa continued to joke.

"We can take care of them. It will be fun."

"*We* can?"

"Certainly. Why not? They're just like any other children. In fact, mother thinks they're always more natural and interesting when they come to the library."

Rosa simply stared. Her big blue eyes were indeed lovely now in her pretty round face, which had lost the flesh which before had all but disfigured it. Her "figger," as she termed her form, was also much more shapely than it had been in early summer, for magical as the result of her simple new living rules really were, there was no denying its reality. Nancy was watching her now with undisguised admiration.

"Yes," she repeated, "it will be fun, and we can get Durand's car—"

"Oh, Nancy, I know!" almost screamed Rosa, "we'll have them here and say they were entertained by Betty, by Mrs. Frederic Fernell! Betty adores that sort of thing and why shouldn't we do it?"

"We'll have to, I guess," said Nancy dryly, "so just come along and prepare Margot."

CHAPTER XXIV

A REAL HOLIDAY

It was amazing how everyone joined in preparing for those children.

"It's so much better fun than just having an ordinary party," Rosa remarked, as she and Nancy folded the paper napkins, "because in doing this we are doing something worth while, and just a party is—only a party," she deduced in her own naive way.

"Yes," added Nancy, "this is more than a party; it's a picnic. And isn't Margot lovely about it?"

"She's going to have the best fun of any of us, for Margot loves children, especially strange children," Rosa said, slyly.

"If only we could get Orilla to come," Nancy continued, "but her mother was away all night and when she reached home this morning Orilla had gone out. I didn't have a chance to tell you that, Rosa," said her cousin. "You were so busy with the baker boy when I got back."

"Oh, I knew you wouldn't locate Orilla. It takes more than a little hunting to do that. She flits around like a squirrel," replied Rosa. "But I'm not worrying about her. We have enough on our own hands now," and she proceeded to count and classify the paper plates.

"But she promised to come and she did seem so dreadfully upset last night," Nancy insisted upon saying. "I'm glad our party will be over early this afternoon. Directly after they leave we must go tell Orilla about the room. I can hardly wait, can you?"

"That was a great idea of yours, Nancy, and so simple. If we had waited to ask Betty and Dad as I thought of doing it would have been ages before we got our answer. But you asked Margot—"

"Margot is in charge here. There always has to be someone in charge of every place."

"So simple when you think; but I don't always think," laughed Rosa. "Won't Orilla be tickled? And why on earth shouldn't she use that old room since it means so much to her?"

"If you'll behave, Rosa," Nancy ventured. "You are not like Orilla, you know; *you* have everything."

"But sense, and you've got the family supply of that."

"Now don't go offending me," warned Nancy. They had little time for this conversation and it was being pretty well mixed up with paper plates and napkins. "You know how unpopular a smart girl is, Rosa," and Nancy dropped her big dark eyes with something like a suspicious blinking.

"Ye-ah, all right, you're a dumb-bell, if you like that better, but I don't know what I'm saying. I can't think of a thing but children. What do you suppose they'll do and say? Think they ever saw a mountain house before?"

"Why, Rosa? How absurd. They're just like any other children, only not so well off. Maybe they'll know more about mountain houses than we do," said Nancy, indignantly.

"That's so. Maybe they go on excursions every week," contributed Rosa. They were ready now to wash up and go to meet the train.

"It isn't likely they go often, because there's such a lot of them to pass the trips around to," Nancy reasoned out.

"Gosh!" ejaculated Rosa. "How you can think!"

"But please don't call me smart, remember how I hate that," again came the warning.

"Don't blame you. Smart girls are a pest and, as you say, unpopular," replied Rosa. "That's one blessing in *my* favor. But don't let's fight about it," concluded Rosa. "Hurry along. We've got to get three cars, you know."

The two girls were wearing their simplest frocks, out of consideration for the coming visitors, but Nancy in her candy-stripe with the red bindings and red belt, and Rosa in her blue chambray, to match her eyes, looked pretty enough and well dressed enough for any picnic.

The bustle and excitement into which Fernlode had been thrown by the girls' sudden resolve, to take over what should have been Orilla's party, was little short of that which goes to make up "a swell affair," as Thomas the butler expressed it, when he insisted upon using the tea carts on the lawn. He knew, he pointed out, how the Fernells did things, and that was the way they were going to be done this time.

Margot claimed that she also knew something of the Fernlode prestige, so she insisted upon a number of things, among them being favors for each guest. These were substantial, as she said, being a half dozen handkerchiefs in a pretty pictured box for each of the twelve children to be entertained.

"And if there's more girls than boys I suppose you and I, Nancy, will have to chip in our best hankies to make up the right kind," cryptically stated Rosa. To which suggestion Nancy merely groaned.

Altogether "the help" as well as the hostesses were enjoying the preparations, and now the girls were racing off to meet the train.

There came, first, the Fernell big open touring car, which Chet the chauffeur drove, then the town car with the three seats which Gar drove, and Dell Durand drove their own touring car, so that provided plenty of room, surely. Two cars would have been ample, but Rosa was afraid "an extra batch" might come, and it would have been dreadful not to have had room enough.

It was really queer to be expecting strangers and not even to know what they would look like, but when the train pulled in, and the conductor began handing children down from the cars, both Rosa and Nancy were too excited to care what they looked like.

Both girls, with Dell, pushed their way to the platform and claimed as many of the youngsters as could be lined up before them.

"I'm Miss Geary," announced the pleasant, stately, middle-aged woman who was in charge of the outing, "and I suppose," she said to Dell, "you are Miss Rigney."

"Miss Rigney is ill," Dell quickly replied,

"but this is Rosalind Fernell and this is Nancy Brandon, both of Fernlode. I'm their neighbor and chaperon," Dell continued in her easy social way. "We'll all do what we can to give you a happy time," she promised brightly.

There was no need for further formalities, and if there had been the girls would have just as completely overlooked the need, for Nancy was trailing off with a quartette of the children, two girls and two boys, while Rosa piloted three girls and one boy. Dell was made custodian of a pair of the "darlingest twinnies," two little girls in blue, and there were also with the party three older girls who assisted Miss Geary.

To attempt to describe a children's picnic would be as futile an undertaking as trying to describe childhood itself, for every moment and each hour something so new and novel developed, in the way of fun and good times, that even a picture of a period in the merrymaking failed to record its actual happy spirit.

"And imagine!" babbled Rosa, while she spilled a whole dish of ice cream by allowing it to slip smoothly off the paper plate, "just imagine a photographer making a picture to be published! Did you notice, Nancy," and she placed a neat pile of dry leaves over the crest-fallen ice cream, "how I looked? Did I look—thin?"

"You looked so happy surrounded by your flock," Nancy assured her, "that weight couldn't count. There, call that curly-head. She hasn't had a balloon of her own yet and she's exploded a half dozen of them. Give her one, Rosa, and tell her—*that's all!*"

They were picnicing and frolicing around stately old Fernlode, and the sight was such a pleasant one that numbers of cars were drawn up, while their occupants witnessed the festivities.

"All our neighbors!" exclaimed Nancy. "There's the Pickerings. Let Thomas bring them cream—"

"And they'll tell Betty! There's the Gormans! Oh, Nancy, why don't we have a big folks party, too?" proposed the over-joyed Rosa.

"No, we couldn't. That would spoil this," Nancy pointed out, having a mind to correct standards. "We must do all we can to have this go off well, and that—"

"Will be plenty," agreed Rosa, steering her tea cart of "empties" (the glasses, cups and real dishes) along the driveway toward the house.

Miss Geary and Dell found each other mutually attractive, their taste for work among children being alike, so that they not only took care of the little ones but had an exceptionally fine time doing so.

"Just look at Margot's face. She hasn't room for all the smiles," Nancy took time to say to Rosa. She was on the lemonade staff and Thomas, the butler, had made the drink pink, "just to make the young ones think of a circus," he explained. That may have accounted for the rush at Nancy's booth, a kitchen table draped with the ends of the vines that formed a canopy above.

At the moment Margot was trying to carry a huge plate of chocolate cake in one hand,

and with the other help little Michael, age five, to navigate toward Nancy's lemonade stand. He had a lollypop in each of his hands, so the leadership was rather difficult to carry out.

How they romped, shouted, sang, cheered and even choked! For the bounty provided this day's outing was plentiful to the point of extravagance.

"Why can't we take them on the lake?" pleaded Rosa again, that offer having been politely refused by Miss Geary a short time before.

"Too risky!" replied Nancy. "But look down at the landing! There are the twinnies all alone!"

"And they're too near the edge," joined in Rosa. "I thought those big girls were watching them. Let's run! They'll topple over—"

But Nancy and Rosa were on their way. The twinnies were in danger and the lake was deep at that point. Innocently the little tots, hand in hand, gazed upon the dazzling water. They seemed fascinated, watching something.

"A flish! A flish!" shrilled little Molly, the fairest of the fair twins.

Then her sister Mattie leaned over—

"Oh!" screamed Nancy. "She's in!"

"It's deep," Rosa warned, seeing Nancy toss off her sweater. But the next moment Nancy jumped into the water and before anyone knew that little Mattie had fallen in, she was promptly fished out! Wet and somewhat scared, the child clung to her rescuer, who easily brought her to shore. It was no trouble at all for Nancy.

"Oh, there's the photographer!" joyfully called out Rosa, and then—

Nancy had to have her picture taken, standing on the end of the landing, with her dripping little friend in her arms. The photographer would call it, he said, "a prompt rescue."

This brought the entire picnic down to the water's edge, and the usual accident had presently been successfully disposed of. There were other incidents, many of them, but they did not prevent the day from drawing to a close. Shadows hovered threateningly near when Margot and Thomas passed around the favors, those pretty handkerchiefs, and the ride back to the station was soon marked as the final treat.

Nancy had changed into a fresh outfit and little Mattie was made happy in the smallest dress that could be borrowed in the neighborhood, prettier than the one she wore before the wetting, which made up for everything to Mattie.

It had been wonderful, that day in all the summer for the Fernlode folks, but Rosa and Nancy had not forgotten Orilla.

"We can go directly from the train to her mother's," Nancy proposed, as they neared the station. "I have a feeling that something is really wrong with Orilla."

"Because she was sick last night?" Rosa asked. They were presently piling the children in the cars and had little chance to talk.

"That and—you know she said she would be here to-day if she were able," Nancy made opportunity to answer. "And I know she meant to keep her word."

CHAPTER XXV

FANTASY

Summer was almost over. It had passed quickly for Nancy, although at first her visit had threatened to be dull, monotonous and even a little unpleasant. But as soon as the conflict between Rosa and Orilla became of concern to her, just so promptly did her own days at Fernlode become absorbingly interesting.

Rosa's worry over a few extra pounds of fat now seemed simply babyish, but so it is with most personal appearance worries. They may mean much to a sensitive girl, but to others they are usually accepted as they should be, as matters of small importance. It is character that always matters most.

All this was clear to Rosa finally, and with it had come the lesson in self-restraint: no candy, the lesson in self-discipline, long walks, and the lesson in common sense: to be sincere. All of which had developed a surprisingly attractive Rosa, and in her laudable cousin's efforts Nancy had enjoyed an active and interesting part.

It had been thrilling—those hunts on the islands, those escapades of Rosa's—and it had been fun when the worry was over. As Nancy repeatedly insisted she would not be called smart, because she wasn't any smarter than most girls; it was simply because Rosa had been so oddly different that Nancy's plain common sense shone forth.

The cousins now were affectionate chums indeed, for trouble and trials often bring forth the brightest flowers of true affection, especially where these troubles do not interfere with the rights of others and are strictly matters which belong in a girl's world.

Having the little picnic proved a welcome change, and its success was marked by many pleasant memories of the children's lovely time, besides the pleasure the report of the affair was sure to bring to Lady Betty.

There remained now but one more problem for the young girls to solve: they must reach Orilla and tell her that Margot had agreed to let her use her old room, under the grape vines, so that she would no longer be compelled to steal in and snatch a few precious moments in her coveted sanctuary.

But where to find Orilla?

Leaving the station Dell drove the smallest of the fleet of cars, with Nancy and Rosa, to hunt for the girl. Inquiring at Mrs. Rigney's they found Orilla's mother in great distress.

"Something must have happened," she wailed. "Orilla has not been home to-day and I've even had the little boys and girls searching the woods for her. Where can she have gone? Do you girls know anything about her?" she implored, excitedly.

Nancy did not say that she too had expected to see Orilla, but the three girls assured the worried mother that they surely would locate her daughter, and once more they faced that almost continuous task of searching the woods.

Driving through the woodland roads at the rear of the lake front, was by no means as easy as sailing on its smooth waters, but this was the way the girls were now compelled to go.

"Those logs she cut down must have been for something," Dell reasoned. "Have either of you found out what she did with those?"

"She intended to build a camp," Rosa answered, "but I don't know where. She was as secretive as a—fox."

"She told me too she had a place in the woods, and spoke of loving the wilderness so much, but she never said anything to me about where it was," Nancy also explained.

"Well, we'll drive along toward Weirs," Dell suggested. "But we can't expect to get out onto the islands from the land side."

Thus they journeyed in the late afternoon, over the rough hills, up and down, in and out, but among the camps picked out along the road, where summer folks had pitched their tents, no sign of Orilla was discovered.

"Could we hire a boat here at this landing and go along the water front?" Nancy suggested. "I feel we must have been near her place that afternoon we helped with the little trees."

"Yes, we could do that," agreed Dell. It was rather late for sailing parties, and the man in the sailor's uniform literally jumped at the chance of taking them on his power boat.

"I believe she is on that island over there," pointed out Nancy, "because when we were on the water that afternoon, I saw a flash of light in that clump of low pines."

"A clue!" sang out Rosa gayly. "Depend upon Nancy to notice things. Tell the man to steer in there, Dell. And let's hope for the best."

Like the other islands this was small in area, and as the girls jumped ashore the boatman took out his "picture-paper" to look that over while he waited, for they all knew the search would take but a comparatively short time.

"Yes, she's been here," declared Rosa, almost as soon as she had stepped on land. "See these bushes? They've just been trampled down—"

"Here's a regular path," interrupted Nancy. "And see all these pieces of paper."

"We are certainly on the trail," agreed Dell. "Nancy, we'll follow you; this was your clue, you know," she pointed out tersely.

Quietly they followed Nancy. The little path was leading some place, certainly, for it was marked out clearly in the heavy grass and undergrowth.

Suddenly Nancy stopped. She felt she was near someone, and the path was opening into a cleared spot that was faced around from the other side with the low scrub pine trees.

"Orilla!" she said, instinctively.

"Nancy!" came a feeble, faint reply.

"Where—is—she!" demanded Rosa, close upon Nancy's lead. "Oh, look!"

There she was, on a bed of pine needles, lying like an Hawaiian under the most picturesque hut. It was open on the side the girls were facing, but the thatched roof fell over the other sides in true tropical fashion.

"Orilla," breathed Nancy, who was quickly

beside the unhappy girl, "what has happened?"

"I'm sick, Nancy," she replied, "too sick to walk and—and—I've been lying here—so long!"

"You want a drink, Orilla," insisted Rosa, all excitement now. "Here's your tin cup, but your water pail is—empty!"

"Yes. I couldn't get to the spring—"

"The boatman may have some drinking water," Dell suggested. "Give me the pail, Rosa."

Immediately they set about to care for the sick girl, stifling their natural curiosity at the strange surroundings.

"Don't go away, Nancy," Orilla begged, as Nancy rose from her side to attend to something. "As I lay here I have been thinking of so many things. Just let me have a drink, Dell. Thank *you* for coming," she said, noticing Dell Durand's kind attention. "I'm not worth all this bother."

"Hush," ordered Nancy, "you don't want

us crying, do you? When folks talk that way—"

"It's so like a funeral," spoke up the impulsive Rosa, who was secretly looking over the hut, mystified and astounded.

"You had better not talk now," Nancy cautioned Orilla.

"Oh, I must; I'm not so very sick, just weak and worried, and I'll be better when I've told you," Orilla insisted. "Girls, this is the camp I was building," she began. "You see, my father was a carpenter and I love even the scent of freshly cut wood."

A smile twisted Rosa's face at this, but she quickly conquered it. She had disastrously followed Orilla in her quest for freshly cut wood.

"Yes, I always carried home chips," Orilla went on, having risen on her queer bed and settled her head against an uncovered pine pillow. "When I was very small I would follow the men who chopped the trees, to carry the chips home in my little sunbonnet. I have always loved new wood."

"This place is wonderful," Dell interrupted. "Just like a picture. I can't imagine you building it all alone. You are really a genius at it, Orilla."

"My arms are very strong—I suppose I've trained them to be," Orilla said, "but Rosa helped me with the wood—"

"You bet I did," exclaimed Rosa, "and my hands still bear the marks."

"Well, you see," the sick girl continued, "I know what an attraction a real hut in a real woods would be, and I've worked at this all summer. I was going to bring parties here—"

"We had one of them to-day," burst out Nancy, and that remark brought on a hurried report of the party just held at Fernlode.

"You did that! You girls!" exclaimed Orilla, who was too surprised to lie still. She was shifting to a sitting position, her thick, bright hair hanging over her shoulders, adding the last touch to her tropical appearance under the thatched hut.

"Why, yes," replied Nancy. "It was the

best fun we had this whole summer. If we hadn't been worrying about you—"

"Why should *you* have worried about me?" Orilla asked, seriously.

"Why shouldn't we?" retorted Nancy.

"Feel better now, Orilla?" Dell inquired. "You see, we have a hired boat—"

"And we've got such glorious news, Orilla," sang out Rosa. "You're coming back to live at our house—"

"I'm—going—back!"

"To your own little room," added Nancy, smiling. "It's all fixed. Margot thought it only fair—"

The color rushed back into Orilla's cheeks as if it had been suddenly lighted there.

"My room! Back to my own—little—room!"

"These little girls are like fairies, aren't they?" Dell interposed. "But not more magical than you have been, Orilla. This place is perfect. Good enough for a fancy picture!"

"If only my mother and her library friends could see it," Nancy commented. "And where ever did you get these queer things? Just look at that East Indian water jug. Isn't it one, Orilla?"

"Yes. I found most of them in a curio shop. I think they came from an old seaman's collection," and the girl on the pine-needle bed smiled. "But how lovely it is to have someone see them besides me!" Orilla sighed. "I had planned this so long and made such a secret of it, I just didn't seem to know how to tell anyone about it. But I'm so glad—now!"

"So are we," declared Rosa. "And I'll tell you, Orilla. You and I had best never have any more secrets Nancy would find them out, at any rate, so what's the use?"

"We must go," announced Dell. "Orilla, do you feel strong enough to walk down to the boat?"

"Oh, yes, I'm much better. I guess I just fretted myself ill, and when I thought no help would come I sort of collapsed."

"Lean on me," commanded Rosa grandly. "You're going to live at our house now, so you will be my guest, sort of," she said humorously.

"I can't believe that," demurred Orilla, and the puzzled look on her drawn face showed how surprised she really was.

Presently they were going toward the boat, Orilla leaning on Dell and Rosa, for she was quite weak and the rough path was not easy to traverse.

"You have fever," Dell said gently. "If we had not found you, what would you have done?"

"Died perhaps," Orilla answered, simply.

"But we were *sure* to find you," Nancy insisted. "Don't you hate to leave your rustic bower? Even your room in Fernlode could never be as lovely as that camp. I've seen pictures like it in the Geographical, but I never expected to visit one in reality," she enthused.

"We'll come back," chanted Rosa, "and bring parties of our own. Won't the boys howl?"

"Step in, please," the boatman ordered, for

they had reached the edge. "It's getting late."

Once seated in the boat the girls did what they could to make Orilla more presentable. They pinned up her hair, fixed the rough khaki blouse, and Nancy insisted upon contributing her tie, although Orilla protested that a tie was not necessary for her to wear, she never did so, she declared. But the bright little tie improved her looks, they were all quite positive of that.

The transfer from boat to auto was made easily, as Orilla, who was perhaps more frightened at finding herself ill and being alone in the camp than actually sick, seemed much better and expressed keen interest in all the girls' prattle.

"Like a real story," Nancy thrilled. "I'll have to tell it hundreds of times to Ted, I know," she laughed happily, for she expected soon to have that welcome privilege.

"Don't let's stop at your mother's now," proposed Rosa. "We can come straight back and fetch her up after you get installed,

Orilla. Margot has been frightfully busy, but she promised to have the room aired and everything," she added sagely.

This plan was quickly agreed upon, and when Dell drew her car up alongside of the porch, Orilla seemed almost too dazed to step out.

"Home, James!" joked Rosa, jumping around gayly. "Fernlode is going to have three girls now instead of just me."

"But I'll soon be going home," Nancy told her, while they all, including Dell, marched along the porch with Orilla.

"Don't mention it, Nancy," begged Rosa. "If I weren't going to school I wouldn't let you go. This way, Orilla. We're going in the front door this time."

"Please don't, I would so much rather not," murmured Orilla. "I love the way I've always gone in—and—I'm sort of nervous, you know."

"Orilla's right, Rosa," Dell replied. "It's much better just to get her quietly into bed.

Don't make the least fuss—" she cautioned aside to the two eager girls.

"Thanks," sighed Orilla. "You see, I can't help feeling a little guilty, Rosa. I did fool you an awful lot." There was the flash of a smile with this admission.

"Not such an awful lot, either," Rosa defended herself, "for all the exercise was surely good for me. See how frail and fairy-like I am!" and she attempted a little demonstration.

"Just open that door, will you?" Nancy ordered. "We'll admire *you* some other time, dear."

Dell had hurried inside to bring the news quietly to Margot, and to tell her of Orilla's weakened condition. Promptly and in her own capable way, Margot slipped into the hidden room, quite as if its blinds had not been closed for so long, or as if the mustiness she had fought for two days to conquer, were merely a new brand of natural perfume.

It took but a few minutes to install Orilla in her bed, which had been made fresh and comfortable, and upon Margot's orders Rosa and Dell then withdrew.

They were really going for Dr. Easton, although they did not let Orilla know that. But Nancy stayed near the sick girl, who seemed still anxious to talk of her secrets.

"The money, you know, Nancy," she said, when Margot had left for some fresh water. "I had saved that to buy the little lot next here."

"Next here?" queried Nancy, again much perplexed at Orilla's statement.

"Yes. There's a strip of land adjoining this. It is only a fisherman's place and he promised to sell it to me very cheap. I had almost enough money, and the fresh-air parties were to pay me more. But I won't need it now. This is—so—much better," and the sick girl sighed happily.

"You were trying so hard to get money to buy land near here," Nancy repeated, beginning to understand Orilla's struggles.

"Yes. It's in the little brown bag, but half

of it belongs to Rosa. She must have it back," Orilla said firmly.

"But I'm sure she won't take it—" declared Nancy.

"Then I'll have to give it to mother. Poor mother, she has worked so hard," Orilla sighed. "But this, having me here again, will surely make her happy."

Dr. Easton found Orilla highly nervous, and privately he told Margot and Mrs. Rigney that the fancied injustice had so preyed upon the girl's mind she had been unable, for the time being at least, to control her bitterness. This would now be removed and so her health would be sure to improve.

Mrs. Rigney had been brought back in the car, as the girls arranged, and in spite of her daughter's illness they were all almost happy.

"It is her dream come true," said Nancy to Rosa. "And she has just given her mother the brown bag with the money. She wanted to give you half."

"I wouldn't take a penny," declared Rosa sharply. "I gave her that and it's all hers."

"That's what I told her, Rosa," Nancy replied. "You won't miss me so much now, you'll be so busy with all this," she pointed out. "I had a letter from mother today—"

"You can't go home—yet," cried Rosa instantly. "You have got to be here when Betty and Dad come. You must know what they say when they see me—thin!"

THE END